Donated to

SAINT PAUL PUBLIC LIBRARY

WITHDRAWN

BOOKS BY DEAN HUGHES

Nutty for President
Honestly, Myron
Switching Tracks
Millie Willenheimer and the Chestnut Corporation
Nutty and the Case of the Mastermind Thief
Nutty and the Case of the Ski-Slope Spy
Jelly's Circus
Nutty Can't Miss
Theo Zephyr

THEO
ZEPHYR

Dean Hughes

THEO ZEPHYR

ATHENEUM   1987   NEW YORK

Atheneum
Macmillan Publishing Company
866 Third Avenue, New York, NY 10022
Collier Macmillan Canada, Inc.

Type set by Haddon Craftsmen, Allentown, Pennsylvania
Printed and bound by Fairfield Graphics, Fairfield, Pennsylvania
Designed by Jean Krulis
First Edition

10 9 8 7 6 5 4 3 2 1

Library of Congress Cataloging-in-Publication Data

Hughes, Dean,   Theo Zephyr.

   SUMMARY: Brad's fantasies, in which an imaginary friend humiliates the bright athletic boy of whom Brad is extremely jealous, start coming true in a way he cannot control.

   [1. Imaginary playmates—Fiction.   2. Jealousy—Fiction]   I. Title.
PZ7.H87312Th   1987   [Fic]   86-28885
ISBN 0-689-31345-4

THEO
ZEPHYR

In memory of
Craig Russel Weight
Who loved to read

ONE:

When the door opened, all the kids looked up. They were supposed to be doing their math assignment, but it was Monday, and any interruption was welcome.

What they saw, however, was something no one could have expected. It was a boy—a strange one—and he was just standing there, grinning. He was short and round-faced, with chubby cheeks. His ears were big, and they stuck out through some loose, rather ragged-looking hair. He was wearing baggy green pants and an old brown shirt that was too big for him. His grin looked silly, his teeth too big for his mouth, and yet, there was something appealing about him, like a dog you like because he's sort of ugly.

All the kids in the class were surprised, but Brad Hill was almost knocked off his chair. He blinked and shook his head the way characters in a cartoon movie do, and then he whispered to himself, "It couldn't be him." But it was. The clothes were different, but that was all. Brad knew that face too well to be mistaken.

Mrs. Hardy said, "May I help you?" She was sitting at her desk on the opposite side of the room.

"Yes, ma'am," the boy said. His voice was surprising—deep and clean, like a radio announcer's. He walked across the front of the room, taking long strides with his short legs, and he stopped near Mrs. Hardy and put his hand out. The other hand was stuck deep in his pants pocket. "I'm Theo," he said. "I assume you are Mrs. Hardy. I'm most happy to meet you—and honored to be one of your sixth-grade students."

That's not his name, Brad thought. *And his voice sounds different. Maybe he's just some kid who looks a lot like . . . but that's his face. I know it is.*

Mrs. Hardy took hold of the boy's hand and gave it a little shake, but she seemed rather mystified. "You're in my class?" she said.

"Yes, ma'am. I've only just arrived in Grandview." The way he said it was strange, as though he meant "just this very minute."

Mrs. Hardy was a person who always knew what to do in any situation, but she acted a little confused right now. The kid didn't let that bother him. He turned toward the class and said, "Allow me to introduce myself. I'm Theo Zephyr. That's spelled Z-E-P-H-Y-R. Zeh-fer. But just call me Theo. Now if you'll each tell me your own name, I promise never to forget."

"Just a moment," Mrs. Hardy said, standing up. "I really think. . . . Perhaps it would be better if. . . ."

Mrs. Hardy was staring. She always told the kids not to stare, but she was doing it herself. And so were all the students, except the ones who were ducking their heads, trying not to laugh. Brad was still blinking. There was no way this could be happening; he really wondered whether he was having some kind of weird hallucination.

"Oh, excuse me, ma'am," Theo said. "I didn't mean to come in and start taking over. I'm afraid I have a tendency to do that. You just tell me when I get out of line."

Mrs. Hardy nodded but said nothing for a moment. She was a gentle woman, pretty, with a nice smile, but she knew how to be firm when she had to be. That's why it was so strange to see her this rattled. "Why don't we step out into the hall for just a moment?" she finally said. "I need to . . . find out more about you."

"Oh, excellent," Theo said. "Wonderful idea. I can always learn the children's names later."

A number of kids started to laugh, but Mrs. Hardy gave them a serious look and then said, "Well, actually, it's fine if you want to learn their names. Students, why don't you each say your name. Cynthia, would you like to start?"

The kids began to announce their names, and Theo listened carefully, sometimes asking to hear one a second time or asking for the spelling. Brad hesitated for just a moment when his turn came, and Theo said, with a big grin, "I know Brad. Brad Hill. I've known him for years and years."

Brad gave his head a quick shake. *Don't do this,* he wanted to shout. But Theo looked to the next person in the row. Brad took a deep breath of relief and looked down, his dark hair falling over his eyebrows. He touched his desk to see if it felt . . . normal. If this was a dream, could everything seem so real?

When all the students had given their names, Mrs. Hardy stepped toward the door, but Theo looked over to the first seat and said, "All right. Cynthia Bauer, Philip Matheson, Carl Zavala, Nancy Price, Steve Bascom, Kerstin Hansen, Jennifer Keith, Jeff Le Duc. . . ." And so he continued all the way around the room. He really didn't seem to be showing off, but he got every name exactly right. Then he turned and said, "Now, Mrs. Hardy, should we have that little chat?"

Not a whole lot of math was done while Mrs. Hardy and Theo were gone. Everyone was whispering back and forth, saying how weird this Theo guy was. But they seemed excited, as though they thought he was going to add a little life to the place.

What if he tells them? Brad was thinking. *Or what if they figure it out? I'd have to move somewhere else. I'd have to run away from home. But it couldn't be him. Things like that don't happen.*

"How do you know that kid?"

Brad looked up. Gil Brimhall was in the next row and a couple of seats ahead, but he was twisting around in his seat. Brad didn't want Gil, of all people, to know. "I don't know him," Brad said. "He must have me mixed up with someone else."

"He knew your name."

Brad tried to think of some explanation. And then he said weakly, "I don't know how he knew me. Maybe he used to live in my neighborhood or something."

"Don't you remember him?"

"No."

"Man, I don't see how you could forget him." And then he added sarcastically, "You two should hit it off. You're about the same size."

Brad was actually bigger—quite a bit bigger—but he didn't say that. He just let it go. Gil thought of himself as such a hotshot; he *would* be the one to start asking questions.

When Mrs. Hardy came back, Theo was right behind her. He commented softly that he liked the way she had decorated the room. "I like daffodils," he said, with that dumb grin still on his face. Brad couldn't believe it. Why was he doing stuff like that? But once Theo sat down at a desk, behind Brad and to the right, he settled in and didn't say a word until recess. Brad looked back at him once, and Theo smiled and waved. After that, Brad didn't look again.

At recess all the kids were eager to find out more about Theo. Several of them crowded around him and started asking questions. He was happy to talk to them, but Mrs. Hardy came along and said, "If you're going to play softball, you'd better get started. Why don't you keep the same teams as last week so you won't have to choose again?"

It had been a cold spring in Utah, and the kids had only been able to play softball for the last few days, even though it was getting to be late in April.

Everyone seemed to agree to keep the same teams, but Gil Brimhall turned to Alan Cuell and said, "You guys have to take that goofy new kid."

"No way," Alan said. "We've already got Merrill on our team, and Betsy—neither one can—"

"Boys, that's enough," Mrs. Hardy said. "Maybe we *should* choose over again if you're—"

"No, that's okay. We'll take him," Gil said, but he obviously wasn't pleased.

As the kids walked onto the field, Theo waited, as though he wasn't sure what he should do. Gil finally yelled over to him, "So what position do you usually play?"

"I'm trying to think. The only time he had me play, I think it was something called central field."

Brad was not far away. He froze. But Gil didn't ask who "he" was. He just said, "It's called *center.* Are you telling me you've only played one time?"

"Well, no. Many times. But it was always the same plays over and over. Except batting. Sometimes I played batter. Isn't that what it's called when you hit the ball?"

Gil was staring. It's hard to say what he might have said if Mrs. Hardy hadn't stepped in. "Gil, that will be fine. Just let him play center field."

"Thank you, Mrs. Hardy," Theo said, even though Gil had said nothing to agree. "I know where that is." Out Theo trotted, his baggy pants and shirt billowing in the breeze as he ran.

Brad waited his turn at bat, standing a little away from the others. He thought maybe he knew what was going on now. And then, when the first batter hit a high fly to short center, he was sure of it.

Theo came loping in a little way and stood under the ball. He made a nice catch with his bare hands. Gil, who had been playing shortstop, had tried to get to the ball, so he was not far away when Theo caught it. He stopped suddenly and took a long look, as though he had just witnessed a miracle. Theo grinned with those big teeth and then tossed the ball to Gil. "That's called an 'out.' Right?"

"Yeah. Way to go."

It was happening. Just the way it always did. But it couldn't be. Brad felt his eyelids to see if they really were open.

They were, and the next play was just the one he expected. The batter was Richard Bills, a small kid like Brad. Gil yelled out in a booming voice, "Move up. Richard can't hit." Gil himself moved in very tight, not all that far from the pitcher. Richard swung a couple of times and missed, and gradually Gil worked in even closer. But on the next pitch Richard hit the ball fairly hard, and it got past Gil before he could react. He stomped his foot in disgust, and then he turned around to see where the ball had ended up.

But there was Theo, about where the shortstop would normally play. He had already scooped the ball up and was firing it to first. Richard was out by a mile.

Theo nodded to Gil and grinned. With those big ears and that crazy hair, he looked like a kid who could never do anything right. But he had just made the best play any of the kids had ever seen, and all he did was turn and trot back to "central" field. Gil spun around and looked at Phil Matheson, who was pitching. "How did he do that?"

"He ran. Didn't you see him?"

"No. I was turned the other way."

"He's the fastest kid in the world. He's got to be."

He'd better not keep this up, Brad was thinking. *They're going to figure out what's going on.* In spite of

Brad's nervousness, however, he was getting some pleasure, too. It was nice to see someone show up Gil. When all this had happened in Brad's mind for the first time, it was just a wish, a daydream like the many daydreams Brad immersed himself in, but seeing it for real like this was a little too good.

The next batter was stepping up. It was Terry Burningham, one of the best hitters. He let a couple of pitches go by, and then he really slugged one. The left fielder took off after it, but he had no chance of catching up. And then Theo came shooting out of nowhere. He was really motoring, those little legs just a blur. The ball seemed to hang in space as Theo closed in on it; then he turned—just the way the major leaguers do—and reached out and caught it with one hand.

Terry had already rounded first base, and he kept running to second, as though he still couldn't accept what had just happened. Gil looked out to left field for a while, and then he turned back and looked at Phil. His eyes were the size of softballs. Theo, meanwhile, was galloping toward the infield, his wild hair blowing straight back. He was waving the ball over his head.

"We get to bat now, I believe," he said as he approached.

"How did you do that?" Gil said.

"Do what?"

"Run so fast. I've never seen a kid who could run that fast."

"Really?" Theo looked curious, as though he had

never thought of such a thing. He looked over at Brad, who was hurrying toward him.

Brad grabbed Theo's shoulder and spun him away from Gil. "Don't do the rest," he whispered.

"Why not? That's how it always ends. I hit—"

"Shut up. Keep your voice down. What are you doing here anyway?"

"What I always do. I don't see what you're getting so upset about."

But Gil was yelling. "Come on, Theo. You're going to lead off. We want to see if you can hit, too."

Brad was doomed. He walked out to right field. This next one was going to push things too far. No one was going to believe it. Whatever satisfaction he had found in seeing Gil look so amazed was going to be lost if. . . .

Sure enough, Theo hit the first pitch out of sight—over the fence, over the street, over the hill, and all the way down into the park below. Nobody could do that. Brad watched the ball sail away, and then he looked back to see what the kids were going to say. But they weren't saying anything. They were staring off at the sky as though they had just witnessed a UFO. Half a minute went by, and no one even moved.

Then Theo said, "Do I run around the bases now?"

Gil looked at him strangely, as though he had been brought back to reality a little too suddenly. "If you want to," he finally said. And so little Theo went zipping around the bases, not putting out much effort but *really* traveling.

When he got back, all the kids were still just standing there, most of them looking at Theo now. The kids in the field had begun to walk toward home plate. Brad, however, was taking his time. Mrs. Hardy eventually said, distantly, "I suppose we'll never find the ball."

"Oh, I'm sorry. I'll retrieve it," Theo said, and he was off again. He glided out to the big chain-link fence, and he scrambled up and dropped down on the other side as if it was something he did all the time, and then he charged across the street and over the hill.

"I'm getting that kid for my summer-league team," Gil said reverently.

"Yeah, if the major leagues don't get him first," someone said.

Then Theo reappeared and ran back across the street. He stopped just beyond the fence and threw the ball all the way to home plate, on the fly. No one even tried to catch it. They watched it bounce away, and then they all looked around at each other. Paulette Chambers said, softly, "No one can throw a ball that far."

Brad felt a chill go through him. How long before the kids figured out what was going on?

TWO:

The rest of the day Theo was hardly noticeable. He seemed very busy with his studies. The other students remained in a state of shock. All day they kept twisting around to look back at Theo, as though they wanted to verify that he really existed. Mrs. Hardy seemed also to be trying to convince herself that everything really was normal, that what she had seen could somehow be explained. "Well," she said at one point, "our new student certainly is a wonderful athlete. We've learned that much about him."

"Thank you, Mrs. Hardy," Theo said, in that big voice of his. "And you're a wonderful teacher. I've enjoyed this day immensely."

Kids weren't even laughing anymore. They all turned around and got another look. What kind of kid was this?

At the end of the day, Brad got to Theo quickly and kept him at the back of the class while everyone else was leaving. "Look," he whispered, "I don't know what you're trying to do, but you've got to get out of here."

"Leave? Already? I've only done one of your day-dreams so far."

"That stuff isn't real. It can't happen in the real world. They'll all figure that out pretty soon."

"Real world? You mean there's more than one world?" Theo seemed quite amazed to hear such a thing.

Brad was without words. Where did he even start? What could you say to someone like this?

Gil had stayed around, and now he came up behind Brad and said, "Hey Theo, I want to talk to you."

"Oh, how nice," Theo said. "I'm hoping to be your friend, if I can. I've seen you lots of times, but I just don't feel I know you very well."

"Seen me? Where?"

Brad spoke quickly. "He just told me he used to live around here. He's watched us play ball and some stuff like that."

"Yes, I suppose that's a way of thinking of it," Theo said thoughtfully, "except that—"

"We'd better get out of here," Brad said. "Mrs. Hardy probably wants to leave."

That was not true. Mrs. Hardy was at her desk, busy with some sort of paperwork. But she took this chance to say, "Theo, could I speak to you for a moment?"

"Certainly. Certainly." He strode to her desk. Brad and Gil waited, and Brad could hear what Mrs. Hardy said, even though she kept her voice down.

"This has been a very strange day, Theo. You sort of took me by surprise. When you came in, I naturally assumed you had been admitted by the principal, and that your parents had come in—all the usual things. But I talked to Dr. Buchmiller this afternoon, and he said he had never heard of you. He didn't get your records or—"

"Tell me about records and I'll see that he gets some."

"Well, you know, the school you came from, birth certificate, proof of residency, test scores—all the things in your file."

"Don't you think I can handle sixth grade?"

"Oh, it's not that at all. It's just the way things are done. You have to come over with your parents and sign in officially. It's not enough just to move into town and show up at a class."

"Ah, I see. I never quite comprehend the way people think about such things. All right. By tomorrow Dr. Buchmiller will say everything is okay."

"Well, fine. But you know he might not assign you to my class. There are two other sixth-grade classes."

"Oh, I see. Well, I'll take care of that too."

"Take care of it? Theo, you can't do that. He's the one who will have to make the decision."

Theo reached out and put his hand on Mrs. Hardy's shoulder. "I like you, Mrs. Hardy," he said. "You'll get used to me. You'll get so you don't mind the way I am."

"I don't . . . mind . . . exactly."

"I'll see you tomorrow." He turned, or rather, spun in place, and took ten giant steps to the door. "Come on, Gil," he said, "let's have that talk."

When the boys got outside, Gil said, "Theo, how would you like to be an Arctic Circle Tiger this summer?"

Theo stopped and turned toward Gil. He looked shocked. "Oh, no. I do people. I don't want to be a tiger."

"What?"

"I don't know how to think like a tiger. I can't picture myself going around like that, on all fours."

"What?"

"Do they even *have* tigers in the Arctic Circle?"

"What are you talking about?"

"No, no, Theo," Brad said. "He means a baseball team. They're called the Tigers. They're sponsored by the Arctic Circle—it's a fast-food place." Then Brad stepped closer and gave Theo a firm look of warning before he turned to Gil. "But Theo told me he's not staying around here very long. He won't be here this summer. In fact, he might be gone really soon."

"How come?" Gil asked, looking at Theo, not at Brad. "Didn't you just move here?"

"Well, it depends on how you think about it. I guess I don't use words quite the same way you do. 'Move,' to me, means—"

"His parents are just thinking about moving here. They might not stay. In fact, it doesn't look like they will."

Some of the other boys in their class had walked over in time to hear what Brad had said. Phil asked, "Where did you used to live?"

Theo thought about that, and Brad held his breath. If Theo said just the wrong thing, and everyone figured out what was going on, Brad was going to look like an idiot.

"I'm never very clear about that," Theo finally said. I suppose you mean 'what place?' Like a city or a town or a country. To me—"

"California," Brad said. "He lived in California most of his—"

"Only on those vacations," Theo said. "Two years ago when you went to Disneyland, and—"

"Let's play some basketball," Brad said. He was in a panic. "Come on. Let's shoot some hoops."

Apparently the other guys had just been heading to do that. Phil had a basketball under his arm.

"Oh, yes. I like that one," Theo said. "Let's do

the one where we play basketball. Gil, you're in it."

"What?"

"Wait a minute," Brad said, and he grabbed hold of Theo and started pulling him away. "Just a second. I've got to talk to Theo."

"Brad, please," Theo was saying. "That's really quite impolite."

But Brad was whispering, "What the heck do you think you're doing?"

"The basketball one on the playground. I can't do the one with the crowd right away. That will take some arrangements."

"Don't do any of them. Get out of here. Just go away now and don't come back."

"But I thought you wanted me to do all this stuff."

"Not out loud. Or, I mean . . . not out where people can watch."

"Brad, I don't know what you're talking about. I don't mean to sound rude, but you really don't make any sense sometimes." Theo walked away, over to the other boys. "Okay, let's form the teams. Gil guards me."

The boys glanced around at each other, obviously baffled, but then they formed two teams of three. Brad was on the team with Theo, since he was also small. By now, they knew enough to expect big things from Theo. All the tall guys—Gil, Phil, and Brian Jorgensen—were on the other team.

What followed was an incredible dribbling and shooting exhibition. It was a one-man show that would put any player on the Globetrotters to shame. At first Theo would fake Gil in the air, dribble past him, and hit the easy lay-up. But pretty soon all three guys were guarding Theo, so he started dribbling between his legs, behind his back, in and out, around and through those guys, and then popping in jump shots from all over the place. He could jump so high he could even out-rebound them when they missed shots.

On defense, he would steal the ball right out of their hands, or if the guys stayed back and tried to shoot from outside, he would block their shots. After about four minutes the score was sixteen to nothing. Brad called time-out. The guys on the other team were standing there huffing and puffing and looking at each other in wonderment. Alan Cuell was just as amazed. He was on Theo's team but had never touched the ball. After the first couple of plays he had just stood there and watched.

"He's pretty good, isn't he?" Brad said and tried to laugh; then he said, "Come here, Theo."

Theo marched away from the others. "Did you see Gil's face?" he asked. "That's what you love—that stunned look on his face. I'll do the big finish on him. That's your favorite."

"Theo, listen to me. No one can play basketball like that. They know that. They're not stupid. If you keep this up, they're going to catch on. If they figure out that I thought all this stuff up, they'll—"

"But I always play basketball like that. I do those same plays every time. Just in different order."

"I know that. But it's just made up. You can't . . . really. . . ." Brad let his breath blow out. This was crazy. He was dreaming. He knew he was. He gave his head a quick knock—but it hurt. "Things like this don't happen, Theo."

"I didn't think you would call me by that name."

"Hey, that's the only thing you've done right so far. If you had used your real name, they would have caught on already."

"You use words in the oddest ways, Brad. You keep changing what 'real' means. Now, come on. I'll do the big finish. You've always loved it before."

There was nothing to say. This wasn't really happening anyway. Brad decided just to follow along and get this over with; then he was going to have to figure out a way to wake up.

Theo took the ball and dribbled steadily, standing in one place. He waited for Gil to come out to cover. Gil was looking determined, unwilling to let this little guy beat him again. Theo dribbled to his right, slowly, allowing Gil to stay close, and then suddenly he did a quick pivot and a behind-the-back dribble, and drove past Gil on the left. Gil was still standing there like a statue. When he finally reacted and spun around, he was just in time to see Theo fly through the air, rotate one hundred eighty degrees, and do a behind-the-head, two-hand slam dunk.

Gil just stood there staring for quite some time,

and then he said, in a voice that was now angry, "You can't do that." Brad didn't know whether to laugh or cry, but he had to admit, it was nice seeing Gil this frustrated.

"I just did," Theo said and smiled in that friendly way of his.

"You're too short."

Theo looked over at Brad. "He's saying strange things too. He's supposed to say—"

Brad dashed to Theo and grabbed him again. "You come with me right now," he whispered, and then, louder, "Well, we'll see you guys later." He was pushing Theo, with his hand in the middle of his back. The two of them were well down the block before Brad dared to look around. All four guys were still standing where they had been. But they were not talking; they were looking up at the basket, as though they were trying to decide whether they had seen what they had seen.

"I think they're on to us," Brad said. "You're talking too much."

But when Brad looked back to Theo, he received the biggest jolt of the day—and he had already had some beauties. Theo was gone. He had simply vanished.

THREE :

Brad really wondered whether he was losing his marbles. By the time he got home he was half convinced that the whole day had never really happened. But if it hadn't, what had? He was relieved to see his mother sitting at the kitchen table, just to know that something normal could happen. Except that it was actually a little out of the ordinary.

"What are you doing home so early?" he asked her.

Mrs. Hill was on a leave of absence from her job

and was going to college, working on her master's degree. Brad usually got home before she did. "I decided to study here this afternoon. It's a lot quieter than at the library."

Brad nodded. He could see she wanted to stay with her books for a while; she was already looking back down at the page. But Brad needed some answers if he could get them. "Mom, was today just a regular day for you?"

"Not really. I've got a test coming up in Dr. Fillmore's class. I've been cramming for that." But for the first time she seemed to notice something. "Is everything okay with you?"

"Sure."

She nodded, but she was still watching him. Mom was a psychology major, and Brad always wondered if she could figure him out. But she was nothing like those psychiatrists in movies, with the German accents and little chin beards. She was small, with dark hair, like Brad's, and quick brown eyes that never seemed to miss anything. "You look a little . . . feverish or something." She reached out and placed her palm on Brad's head.

Brad stepped back. "I'm not sick. I'm okay." He started to walk out of the kitchen. But he was still wondering. "Mom, can strange things happen to regular people?"

"Like what?"

"I mean, do normal people ever see things that couldn't really be there?"

24

"Why? What did you see?"

"Oh, I didn't. I don't mean me. I just wondered, you know, if stuff like that can happen."

"What kinds of things are you talking about?"

She looked suspicious. Brad decided to drop the whole matter. "Oh, I don't know. Never mind. You go ahead and study."

"I'm really not sure what you mean, Brad. Normal people can have hallucinations. Illness, high fever, dehydration, lack of sleep, alcohol, drugs—quite a few things—could make someone see something that wasn't really there."

Brad nodded, thinking about that. He knew it couldn't be most of those things. "You mean, like if you didn't drink enough water, you could start freaking out and—"

She was laughing. "No, honey. You'd have to be dying of thirst and maybe overcome with heat."

Brad hadn't been particularly thirsty. He didn't think that could be it. "Don't crazy people see things that aren't there?"

"Sure. That's basically what psychosis is. People have all sorts of delusions. They think they're some-one they're not, or they hear voices, or they imagine various things."

"And they're nuts, right?"

"Well, I think it might be better to use my word, psychosis, or to say they're mentally ill."

Maybe that's what he had. Psychosis. He almost asked how a kid could get it, but he decided he had asked enough. Mom was going to start pushing this thing if he wasn't careful. He started to walk out of the room again.

"Brad, I'm not sure what you're talking about, but remember, kids have great imaginative power. And that's good. Pretending, fantasizing, making things up—that's just playful, and that's okay. If you have a friend who has a rich imagination, you don't have to start thinking he has mental problems. It might just mean he's creative. Some really brilliant kids get so bored with school that they invent fictions, just for entertainment."

"Thanks, Mom. That's good to know."

"Is that what you were wondering about?"

"Sort of, I guess. Something like that." Brad got out of there, and he went upstairs to his room. Maybe that was it. Maybe he had a rich imagination. Maybe he was creative. Maybe he daydreamed all that stuff just to avoid boredom. But brilliant he wasn't; he was sure of that. If he was, why did Gil always get higher grades on everything? And anyway, why didn't it all seem like a daydream? It still seemed so real.

The thought of Gil gave him an idea. He wanted to make sure this whole day had really happened. He looked up Gil's phone number and then called him. Gil's little sister answered, and it took quite a while before Gil got to the phone. He puffed out a "hello" when he answered, sounding out of breath.

"Hi Gil, this is Brad."

There was a long pause and then, "Yeah?"

"What are you doing?"

"Why?"

"Oh, I don't know."

"Look, what do you want?" He definitely sounded mad. What did that mean?

"Ah . . . the math assignment."

"What math assignment?"

"Didn't Mrs. Hardy give us a math assignment?"

"No. You know that. She gave us time to do it in class."

"Oh, yeah. I forgot."

A pause again, and then, "Is that all you wanted —or did you want to rub it in some more?"

"Rub what in?"

"About the basketball game. Don't be cute."

He still hadn't said it—not entirely. Maybe it wasn't what Brad thought. Carefully, he said, "You mean about Theo?"

"Yeah, I mean about Theo. There's something that's not right about that kid, Brad. Something's going on. I asked my dad, and he said no kid that tall could jump that high. It's not even possible."

"Did you see him jump that high?"

"Yeah. Sure I did. He stuffed the ball. You saw it."

Brad forgot to say good-bye. He just put the phone down. It was true then. Either that or he had just dreamed up this phone conversation. Either way he was probably crazy, because the whole thing couldn't possibly be real. "I do have psychosis,"

Brad mumbled to himself. "I hope it's just the twenty-four-hour kind." That was his own little joke, but he wasn't laughing.

The next morning Brad's "illness" hadn't gone away. There was Theo at his desk. And everyone else was talking to him, even Mrs. Hardy. Whatever sickness Brad had was going around.

When he got a chance to speak to Theo alone, Brad walked back to Theo's desk, leaned over, and whispered, "Please leave, okay? Please. I can't take having you around another day."

"Brad," Theo said, "what an unkind thing to say. Besides, you can't have me and not have me. You have to make up your mind about that."

"Oh, yeah? Well, what if I punch your lights out?"

"What lights, Brad? I don't think I have any lights, do I?"

But now Mrs. Hardy was asking Brad to sit down. He did, but he feared the worst. What was Theo going to come up with next? He tried to remember all the things he had dreamed of Theo doing. Most of them were awful—too embarrassing to think about. Even if the kids never figured out what was going on, Brad was embarrassed to admit to himself that he had made up such corny stuff.

It wasn't until later, during math, that Brad saw what was coming next. Theo volunteered to demonstrate a problem on the chalkboard, and as soon as he started walking to the front of the class, Brad remembered what was about to happen. He ducked his head and prepared himself for the worst.

Sure enough, Mrs. Hardy read off the problem, and a quick scrape of chalk followed. Brad looked up to see the answer written on the board—no problem, just the answer.

Mrs. Hardy was staring again. "Well, Theo, that is correct," she finally said. "But could you show us how you arrived at the answer?"

"Oh, I'm sorry. I'd be happy to." He erased the answer, and then suddenly his hand began to move so fast it became a blur. In about three seconds the problem—with all the computations and the answer—was on the board. Mrs. Hardy was nodding very slowly. The class was silent, everyone looking at the board, verifying that he really had done the problem.

"That's amazing," Mrs. Hardy said, her voice hardly audible. "Try this one." She gave him another problem, a harder one. A blaze of hand movement followed, and then, quick as a calculator, the answer appeared. She gave him three more, and each time it took Theo longer to erase the old problem than to solve the new one.

Brad glanced over at Gil, who was watching intently, his jaw set. It didn't take a genius to see that Gil didn't like this. He had always been the best student, as well as the best athlete, in the whole grade. Everyone had known that for years. But now, this new little guy was taking over.

Brad found a certain satisfaction in seeing Gil's face, but he knew what was coming, and it was . . . unthinkable. Somehow Theo had to have the mercy not to go through with it.

But Theo was going through the whole routine. He did a problem, a huge one, with numbers running all over the board. He was like those math geniuses, the college professors, you hear about. The numbers and symbols flowed from his chalk like water from a hose. And then came the stupid part—the incredibly stupid part. Mrs. Hardy suddenly jumped up and ran to Theo, threw her arms around him, and kissed him on the cheek. "You're the most wonderful student I've ever had," she said. "It's a fabulous joy just to have you in my class. You put Gil to shame."

Brad had lowered his head and cupped his hands over his ears, but it had all come through. And yet, he knew it just couldn't happen. Mrs. Hardy would never do that. She was so pretty and so nice, and Brad liked her better than any teacher he had ever had. Now he felt like it was his own fault that she had done such a thing.

He peeked at her. Mrs. Hardy was suddenly humiliated, obviously wondering why she had acted that way. She was already searching for words, trying to think of how to apologize, especially to Gil. Theo was nodding at Brad, with a look of great joy on his face.

This was something worse than psychosis. This

was the whole world gone crazy. Brad wanted to dig a tunnel out of the universe and not return until someone made everyone start playing by the old rules. The softball and basketball games had been sort of fun, but this was just stupid.

But here was Theo on his way back to his desk, giving Brad a thump on the shoulder. "I like that one better than the one about the best English paper," he whispered, all too loudly. "But I can do that one another time if you want me to."

"No," Brad mumbled. "No."

FOUR:

All day Brad expected other things to happen, but Theo was pleasant and friendly to everyone and did nothing out of the ordinary. At recess, as the boys were walking out of the building, however, Brad warned Theo not to play softball the way he had the day before. Theo said he only knew one way to play; he was sorry.

"Then come with me," Brad said. "Right now."

Brad looked both ways and then said, "Come on, before Mrs. Hardy gets out here." He grabbed

Theo by the arm and more or less pulled him across the street to the concrete stairs that led down the hill and into the park below. He didn't let go of Theo's arm until they had reached the bottom.

"I know this is against the rules," Theo kept saying. "We're not supposed to leave the playground."

But Brad didn't care right now. Some of the kids might have seen them go, but he was willing to take that chance. He stopped at the bottom of the stairs and turned to Theo. "All right. Now this is it. I made you up, so I'm your boss. I want you to go away and never come back. And I want you to leave right now —just the way you did yesterday."

Theo stared up at Brad for several seconds. He looked hurt. "You don't mean that," he finally said. "I've just been doing the things you always have me do."

"I just imagined that stuff. I didn't want it really to happen."

Theo looked confused. "If you imagined it, it did happen," he finally said.

"No. Now that's the problem here, Theo. You seem to think that stuff that happens in a person's mind is the same thing as stuff that happens on the outside. And I think that's how you got mixed up and came outside where you don't belong. I'm not crazy. You're just lost."

Theo smiled a little at that. Then he sat down on the stairs. "I like to listen to you talk sometimes," he said. "You make words do whatever you want them to do. It's as if you make up the world as you go along."

"Theo, I don't know what you're talking about. I'm not making anything up now. I was making things up when I used to think about you. But I'm not going to do that anymore. I'm going to shut you out of my head forever. But first you have to leave."

This really cracked Theo up. "Oh, sure," he said. "How am I supposed to walk away? You're forgetting that I don't even exist unless you think me."

"Well, then . . . do what I say. I'm in charge here."

But this only set Theo off, making him laugh all the more. "Brad, Brad, you're going to break me in half, the way your mind is working. You can't create someone and then just cancel him out with a few words. How would you like to get wiped out that way?"

"That's not at all the same thing."

"And why isn't it?"

"Because I'm real, and you're not."

"Oh, sure. Throw that up to me."

"Well, I can't help it. It's true."

"Yes, to you. You're the one who split the world in half and then named one part real and the other part unreal. It's just another one of those word tricks you like to do."

"Theo, you're nuts. I didn't make the world that way. It's always been that way. There are real things you can touch. And there are ideas. One is real and one isn't. Everyone knows that. I didn't make you into an idea. That's just what you are."

"You did too make me into an idea."

Brad blew his breath out. He was caught on that one. He had to regroup his ideas—the ones that weren't walking around outside his head—and see what he could do to explain what was what to this little guy.

"Look. I know I made you into an idea. But that's the only thing I could do. I couldn't make you into a real person. Now I wish I hadn't thought you up at all."

"Why did you then?"

"I don't know. When I was little, I guess I wanted to have a friend to play with, so I liked to think about you. We talked and played and stuff, and I had you do all kinds of neat things. Sometimes I still like to think about you, to imagine what it would be like to do things that you can do—that's all."

"Sometimes?"

"Okay. Quite a lot. But I've learned my lesson. I don't want to think about you anymore. The things you do are too embarrassing. And if you keep saying some of the stuff you say, the kids are going to figure out who you are, and everyone's going to know what stupid stuff I think about. That would just kill me. You can understand that, can't you?"

"No."

"No? Why not?"

Theo leaned back on the stairs and put his hands

behind his head. He cocked one foot up over the other knee. He was still wearing the same goofy clothes he had worn the day before. Brad had never thought of him dressed that way. Sometimes Theo did things his own way, whether he admitted it or not. "I don't understand things, Brad. I didn't learn them, or find them out, or something like that. I just know them. The trouble with you is, you think with all those words of yours, and it makes you confused. Most of the time you know what you *think* but you don't know what you *know*."

"Theo, you talk in riddles. That doesn't even start to make sense."

Theo giggled. "Oh, Brad, you are fun to talk to. I'll say that." He looked off into the distance and seemed to enjoy the moment. "Words. They don't work very well, do they?"

"Not the way you use them." Brad dropped down on the grass near the stairs and folded his legs under him. He was in the mood to give up. Theo wasn't going to listen to him anyway. He was going to do whatever he wanted to do.

"Brad, I'll get you started in the right direction. I'll tell you one thing you know—and you can go from there."

"Oh, this is cute. *You* are going to tell *me* what *I* know."

"Excellent. That's the best sentence I've ever heard you say. And now, here it is: You know that you want me to stay, or I would already be gone."

"No. No way. That's not true. Maybe once I *did* want you. But now I don't. It's that simple."

"That's a strange thing to say, Brad. Things do not exist and then stop existing so easily as you think."

"You mean I'm not allowed to change my mind?"

Theo suddenly looked delighted. "What a wonderful idea," he said. "Change your mind. But I don't know where you'd get a new one. And besides, with a new one you wouldn't know what you know any better than you do with this one."

"Lay off, Theo. That's not what I meant." Brad dropped over on his back, flat on the grass. This was all too much. He couldn't talk to this guy. "Theo, just go. That's all I ask. Just go away. I know things can go away. Last year David Patzke moved away, and I've never seen him since."

Theo laughed. "Yes, and as a little boy, you hid your head under a pillow and thought no one could find you."

"That's not the same." Brad sat back up before Theo could respond. "Look, just stop doing the things I used to think about. That's all I'm asking you."

"Ah, now that's another matter. As you said before, you are my boss. I can't do what I do unless you think what I do. You think; therefore, I am."

"Okay. Let's make a deal. I won't think that stuff anymore, and you don't do it."

"That's fine with me."

"Really? Do we have a deal?"

"Of course. That was always the deal. It's just that you haven't been able to do your part, so I have to do my part."

"I will now. I'll stop thinking about all that stuff."

"Brad, listen to me. You're trying to kid yourself. There are things that you know. And once you let yourself know that you know them, I won't be able to continue. It's as simple as that."

"What do you mean—what things do I know?"

"You know everything. It's all inside you. You just have to listen to yourself."

"Theo, that's crazy. I don't know everything. I hardly know—"

"Everyone knows, Brad. They know everything. They just look in the wrong direction."

"Theo, that's just a bunch of mumbo jumbo to me. I can't even figure out what you mean."

"Don't figure it out. Just know."

"Well, what if I can't do that?"

"You can. But if you don't, things will not change with me. I thought tomorrow might be a good time for the last-second shot, and then maybe I'll do the lion after that. And then we'll do some variations if you like. Or we can go straight to the big one—you know the one I mean."

"Oh, no," Brad said, and he dropped back on the grass again. "I'll die if you do that stuff. It's embarrassing and stupid, and it's . . ." Then Brad realized which one Theo meant by the "big one." "No,

Theo, you can't do that one. I never really felt good about that one, not even when you were doing it."

"I don't know how to think about that, Brad. I just know what we do. And I have said all I have to say for now. Should we go back to the school?"

Brad jumped up. "Oh, geez. How long have we been down here? If the class has gone back in, we're in real trouble."

"Don't worry. None of your time has passed. We've been on my time, not yours."

Brad had no idea what that meant. He had no idea what much of anything meant anymore. The only thing he was sure of was that if Theo did the last-second shot tomorrow, it would be the worst day of his life. And if he did those other things . . . oh, wow . . . Brad didn't know a mess could get this big.

And then, suddenly, Brad and Theo were on the sidewalk, just outside the school. They didn't even have to climb the stairs. But Brad was too worried to find any joy in that. He turned to Theo. "Give me a day, okay? Don't play baseball, or basketball, or any of that stuff. Just be normal."

"I only have so many things I do, Brad. You really haven't given me much variety."

"Well, you can sit in school and keep your mouth shut, can't you?"

"Yes, of course. But never for very long. You always have me running off to—"

"Okay, I know. But take a day off."

"Okay. Fine. I can use the rest."

Brad and Theo turned to walk toward the playground when someone called to them. Gil and Alan were running across the lawn toward them. "What the heck is going on?" Gil said, still at a distance.

"What do you mean?" Brad asked.

Gil jogged to a stop. He and Alan both looked strange, as though they had just experienced a terrible shock. "We came out of the school and turned the corner, and no one was around, and then—wham!—you two appeared out of nowhere."

Brad couldn't think of what to say. He stammered for a moment and then finally said, "We were just walking along here. You must not have seen us."

"No way," Alan said. "We both saw it at the same time. You just . . . materialized—like people in a science-fiction movie."

Brad glanced at Theo, who was grinning hugely. He looked ready to say something, so Brad jumped in. "Think about it," he said. "Could that happen? How could we just appear all of a sudden?"

"I don't know," Gil said, "but I know what I saw. And just when it happened, Alan said, 'Did you see that?' He saw the same thing."

"It was probably the sun in your eyes or something."

"Then how come you're acting so weird?"

"Weird? I don't know what you're talking about."

"Yes you do. You're acting scared—as if you're afraid we're going to find out something."

Brad tried to act casual. He forced a laugh. "Look you guys, you're the ones acting weird. You're the ones seeing things. There's one thing I know for sure—people don't just appear and disappear."

He looked over at Theo, who was still grinning.

FIVE:

Brad used Theo's "day off" to think. He tried all afternoon, especially after school, to get a handle on what Theo had been talking about, but he got nowhere. He was tempted to see what his parents thought, but he was hesitant to get their curiosity going. He waited until dinner, even waited until he was almost finished, and then he couldn't resist. "Dad," he said, "do you think people actually know everything—and maybe just don't know they know it?"

"What's that?"

Somehow Brad knew this was a mistake, but he was desperate. "Do you think that we all, somehow, know everything, but don't know we know it, so we go around thinking we don't know it when we do?"

Dad just looked at Brad for several seconds, and then he looked over at his wife. "Eileen, I think this job is for you. You're the shrink. See what you can do for your poor son—he's finally flipped his lid."

"Just answer him, for heaven's sake." But Mom was smiling, if only just a little.

"All right. I can do that." Dad took another good long look at Brad. "No," he said, and he paused again. "Does that take care of it for you?"

Brad nodded. He was going to let it go. He knew his dad was kidding him, but he also knew he wasn't going to get an answer.

"What ever gave you such a crazy idea?"

"I don't know. I just wondered."

"George," Mom said, "why should he ever ask you a question if you won't even take it seriously?"

Dad looked at his plate for a moment, and then he took a deep breath, as though he were trying to get up his energy. "All right. That's certainly true. I'll show the boy what a fine father I am." He nodded slowly, pretending to be deep in thought. "I can't remember the capital of Delaware, so I don't know everything. I am almost sure that I am not alone. Does that answer your question?"

Brad decided to drop the matter. Dad was not the

sort of guy who liked to speculate about things. He liked to keep things simple.

"Well, now wait a minute," Mom said. "If you once knew it, it's stored in your mind somewhere. It might be correct to say you know it but don't know you know it."

"Okay, I'll put it another way," Dad said. He slid his chair back from the table rather briskly. He was not a big man, but he did things in such strong ways that he always seemed rather sizable. There was a hint of a smile on his face; this sort of thing was Dad's idea of fun. "I've got a guy who works for me down at our plant, and he doesn't even know Delaware exists. I'm not entirely sure he knows Utah exists—and he's lived here all his life. So he doesn't know everything. In fact, he knows very close to nothing. Case closed."

He flashed a little grin at his wife, tucked some stomach under his belt, picked up his newspaper, and walked to the door. "Brad, next time you have another tough question, just come to me. Mom will just get you confused." Again the grin, and he was gone.

But Mom ignored him. "What are you talking about, Brad? Obviously, no one knows everything. But I'm not sure you mean exactly that."

"I'm not sure what I mean either," Brad said. He slid his own chair back, but with no force at all. "If someone really smart—the smartest person you'd ever met—said that, what do you think he would mean?"

"Tell me exactly what it was again."

"We all really know everything. We just don't know what we know. He even said we shouldn't think so much—just know."

"And who was this?"

"Just a guy."

"At school? Or where?"

"Yeah. Or, no. I mean . . . I think it was on TV or something. I just heard it somewhere."

Mom was watching Brad carefully, those sharp eyes of hers scanning his face. "You're acting strange again today, Brad. Why don't you just tell me what's going on?"

"Hey, I just asked a couple of questions, that's all."

"Strange ones."

Brad shrugged. It was time for another exit.

"Listen, Brad. Just a minute. Maybe the person meant that we know a lot more about *ourselves* than we admit. We may not know all the objective facts of the world, but we have lots of information about ourselves that we may be denying. We may have certain feelings—maybe fears—that we don't like to admit. They're in our unconscious mind, but we don't acknowledge them, so we don't know our own feelings. Maybe this person, whoever it was, meant something like that."

"Yeah, I guess." Brad stood at the door for a few

seconds, trying to decide whether to leave or not. "But it seems like Dad's right. If you don't know it, you don't know it."

"Sure. But there are things you know that have never become what we call 'cognitive'—things you've never really said to yourself."

Brad nodded, and then he let it go. He went up to his room. Maybe Theo meant something like that. But he doubted it. Theo didn't think like anyone else.

All the same, Brad thought a great deal that evening, not so much about what Theo had said, but about all the things he had dreamed up over the years to have Theo do, especially the things that made Gil look bad. Most of that stuff bothered him now. He really didn't want it to happen. Why couldn't Theo believe him about that?

When morning came, Brad was more frustrated than ever. He hadn't made any real headway the night before, and now Theo was probably going to go ahead with one of Brad's daydreams. Brad really needed somehow to show Theo who was boss. Maybe it was a matter of taking control, getting a grip on his own mind by getting firm with Theo. In fact, maybe that's what Theo expected.

All the way to school, Brad practiced being firm. He thought of things to say to Theo. He even gave a shot at stopping Theo's existence by unthinking him. That didn't go very well. Theo kept sneaking in through the back alleys of his brain.

But as Brad reached the playground and headed across it to the school, suddenly Theo was standing there in front of him. "Hello. You wanted to talk to me?" He had that dumb, big-toothed grin on, as if he thought it was hot stuff to spring up on a guy like that.

Brad spun around to see whether anyone else had seen Theo appear. There were some other kids around, but no one seemed to be paying any attention. "Come here," Brad said, and he walked Theo out to the middle of the softball field where no one would come by and overhear them. "I'm taking control of my own thoughts. You said yourself, I'm the one who has to do that. I command you to disappear and never return."

"Brad, you know you would miss me in five minutes. You would be thinking me right back, just as always."

"No, I wouldn't. I've had enough of you this time. I'm going to count to three, and when I get to two, you'd better be gone." Brad had heard some tough guy say that on TV.

"What will you do if I'm not?"

"You'll find out."

That stupid grin was so maddening. "One. I'm not kidding, Theo. This is it. I'll give you to three and that's it. Two."

"You're still telling yourself that I'm the one who has to leave, when it's you who has to make me go."

"All right—three, and that's just what I'll do."

Brad suddenly reached out to grab Theo, but Theo dodged a step to the left and was still there. Brad lunged at him and came up with air again.

"That's silly, Brad. You can't get rid of me that way."

"Then I'll do it this way." Brad doubled up his fist and edged carefully toward Theo, watching him for the slightest move. Suddenly he lashed out at Theo's face.

But Theo's head moved far too fast. "Brad, this is you at your very worst. Why do you resort to such tactics? You know much better."

"Stand still and fight me, you gutless little runt."

"Is that what you want, Brad? Do you want me to hurt you? You know what I can do."

"Not to me you can't." He threw a hard punch again, right at Theo's nose. But Theo's hand was there. He caught Brad's fist and stopped it, and then he began to squeeze. Gradually, his grip tightened until it hurt, and then in another few seconds Brad couldn't stand it. He dropped to his knees. "Let go," he said. "Come on. Let go."

"You're doing it again, Brad. I give you what you ask for, and then you say you don't want it."

Brad was gasping. "Not to me. I don't want you to do this to me."

With Brad on his knees, Theo did let go. "Brad, do you see it now? Do you know what you know? You can't just direct such things outward. They come back."

Brad got up. "I thought I could show you who the boss was," he said. Now he sounded rather meek.

"You are the boss," Theo said. "I told you that before. But you can't use tricks. There's no short-cut."

"Don't do the basketball game yet, okay? Give me another day."

"I can't do that, Brad. I'm going to set up the game for this afternoon."

"The one that Gil is in?"

"Yes. I just have to arrange for another team, cheerleaders, referees, and all those sorts of things."

"Theo, you can't do that. It's not basketball season, and we don't have school teams anyway. Some guys from our school played in a city recreation league, but that's all over now. There's no way you can just create a game out of nothing."

"You always do. What's basketball season anyway?"

"It's the time when you play basketball. It's mostly in the winter. It's been over for at least a month."

"What a strange idea."

"Maybe to you, but that's how it is. And I hope you just noticed—you don't know everything."

Theo grinned, his cheeks bunching into little round balls. "Since basketball can be played any-time, there cannot be a season for it. You're the one who is confused. It's just as dangerous to think you know—when you don't—as it is not to know."

Brad made a quick decision to change the subject before Theo trapped him. "Well, tell me this. What's the capital of Delaware?"

"What's a capital and what's a Delaware?"

"See. You don't even know. Delaware's a state."

"A state of what?"

"Not a state *of* something. It's a state in the United States."

"Ah, yes. You people like to divide space into parts and give the parts names, don't you?"

There was no winning in a conversation with Theo. Brad decided to quit talking, but for once a little hope was developing in the back of his mind. Finally, Theo's lack of knowledge just might stop him. He could twist things around if he wanted to, but he couldn't get up a basketball game when it was almost May, and no teams were even playing. And he couldn't get cheerleaders when the school didn't even have any.

Theo, of course, ignored this advice and walked into school, straight to Mrs. Hardy's desk. Brad sat down at his own desk and couldn't help smiling. The bell was going to ring any minute now, and poor Theo was going to be sent to his seat. Mrs. Hardy would tell him that organizing basketball games was not something sixth-grade students did during schooltime.

He watched the conversation, although he

couldn't hear what the two were saying. Mrs. Hardy had lots of questions, and Theo was talking in that happy, confident way of his, his head bobbing as he spoke.

And then she was writing a note for him, and Theo was leaving the room. What the heck was going on?

Theo was gone all during math. Brad hardly got a thing done. What was Theo trying to do? If he was talking to the principal, he was getting his lunch eaten, that's what he was doing. Dr. Buchmiller was a no-nonsense guy who would explain to Theo in no uncertain terms that. . . .

There was a crackle on the intercom, and then Dr. Buchmiller's voice came through the speaker at the front of the room. "Students and faculty, I have an announcement I think will please you. This afternoon at two o'clock you will be dismissed from classes to go to the gym, where the boys from our sixth grade will play a basketball game with the boys from Westridge school. Will all the boys who played on the Grandview Grizzlies city recreation-league team please come to the office at this time."

Gil got up, grinning, and he looked over at Phil. Alan Cuell also slid out of his desk. The three glanced around, taking in all the glory they could, and then they strutted from the class.

Brad's breath caught. It was no longer surprise he was feeling. All along he had feared that Theo might find a way. What bugged him right now was watching those guys. They were going to play in front of the whole school, and they were loving it. He hated the thought that he was giving them this chance.

Theo came back after a while, and he gave Mrs. Hardy a note. She read it, and then she asked two of the girls in the class to go to the office. Brad had no idea what that was about, and the girls didn't seem to know either.

Theo made a point of walking past Brad as he walked to his seat. He was grinning, obviously very satisfied with himself. "How did you do it?" Brad whispered.

Theo shrugged. "The same way you always do, I guess. How do you do it?"

Never mind. Brad slid down in his desk and shut his eyes. He tried one last time to blank Theo out of existence. He gave it a full minute—an attempt at total blackness, the absence of Theo. But when he opened his eyes and looked, Theo gave him a grin and a wave, as though he knew what Brad had been up to. It was hopeless.

SIX:

When two o'clock came around, everyone was dismissed from class to go down to the gym. And there were the boys—in new uniforms. Not the little rec-league shirts they usually wore, with various colored trunks, but classy brown and gold, color-coordinated suits just like the pros wear.

And then Brad got the big shock. There were six cheerleaders out there, all girls from the sixth grade, and they had on beautiful outfits. They were already getting the crowd excited, doing cheers they had learned somewhere. They looked like they had been practicing for years. And one of them was Kathy Noyes. Brad suddenly felt almost sick. He was pretty sure he knew which ending Theo was going to put on this thing. Why did he have to choose the stupidest one?

Brad stayed down at the end of the bleachers, near the door. He wanted to see. He couldn't resist that, but he was going to be the first one out the door when the game ended, especially if Theo put in that last part.

The whole thing was unbelievable. At any minute he expected people to start catching on that it couldn't really happen. There were real referees, with striped shirts, an announcer, and an official timekeeper. The students were up there in the stands doing cheers as though they had known them all along. Didn't it even occur to them that they had never learned any of that stuff? If Theo ever said the wrong thing in front of others, everyone would put two and two together and come up with Brad as the source of all this stuff.

Somehow the coach was there—one of the kid's dads. But he seemed to know what was going on better than he had during the regular season. He had the players doing fancy warm-up drills, and he had a clipboard he kept referring to. How had he managed to get off of work? Had Theo arranged that too? It was crazy.

Just as crazy, but not very surprising, Theo had

also somehow managed to get himself on the team. There he was, out there warming up. He had never worked out with these guys, not even once, and yet he seemed to know the drills. He was popping in some fancy shots too, and the kids were all talking about him.

Brad saw Scott Harward come into the gym. Scott had been in his fifth-grade class the year before, and they had been fairly good friends for a while. Brad watched Scott's face, and saw the amazement. Then Scott glanced up and saw Brad, and he did what Brad hoped he wouldn't: He came up and sat down next to him.

"Can you believe all this stuff?"

"No, I can't," Brad said, meaning something different from what Scott had meant.

"Why are they making this into such a big deal? We never had anything like this before."

"I don't know."

"Everyone's saying this new Theo kid got it all arranged."

"I don't know. Maybe he did."

"Did he really do a slam dunk the other day?"

"Who told you that?"

"Gil. Isn't Theo supposed to be a friend of yours? That's what Gil said."

"I don't know why he said that. I don't know him."

"What's the matter? Are you mad or something?" Brad didn't even answer, just gave a little shrug. "I know one thing. It's about killing you to see old Gil out there showing off."

"Who cares?"

"You do. I know how much you hate him."

"I don't hate Gil. I don't care what he does."

"Oh, sure. I remember last year when you worked so hard on that science project, and then Gil brought in that big fancy display—that thing on erosion or whatever it was—and Mr. Cowles made such a huge thing out of it. You were so mad you wouldn't even talk the rest of the day."

Brad had nothing to say to that. He hated even remembering it. "Well, watch him make a fool out of himself today. He thinks he's the great basketball star, but he'll be so bad today the crowd will be booing him before the game's over."

Scott gave Brad a strange look. "How do you know that?"

"I just think that's what will happen."

"I doubt that. He's the best player in the school."

"He thinks he is."

"Look Brad, I don't like Gil that much either. But he is a good basketball player, and he's probably the smartest kid in the school too."

"So what? He also *thinks* he's the biggest hotshot who ever lived."

"Yeah, well, sometimes he can be all right."

Brad didn't respond. Scott waited a minute, and then he said, "Should we go closer to the middle, where we can see better?"

"Go ahead. I want to sit down here."

"Okay. See you later." But as Scott got up, he looked back at Brad, as if to say, So what's wrong with you?

Brad didn't care; in fact, he was relieved. He wanted to be alone. He was dreading the stupid ending of this thing, and he was afraid of what Theo might say afterward. All the same, there was something he wanted to see. He never exactly admitted to himself what it was, but he knew.

The game went just the way it was supposed to. Theo wasn't a starter. He looked like a first-grader sitting on the bench with all the tallest guys in the sixth grade. But he was all decked out in his fancy warm-up suit, and he kept looking around to spot Brad. Whenever Gil would make a mistake, he would look around and grin.

The Grandview team didn't play all that badly, but they were inconsistent. They would get a couple of points ahead and then drop behind by a few. Most of the guys were playing better than usual, but most often it was Gil who messed up. Just when his team would build a little lead, Gil would throw the ball out of bounds, or double dribble, or take a really bad shot. But the coach left him in the game no matter what he did.

Early in the second half, some of the kids in the crowd started chanting, "We want Theo. We want Theo." Soon all the Grandview fans picked it up. But the coach paid no attention. Even the players begged him to put Theo in, but it was no dice. *Oh, geez, this is so stupid,* Brad thought. It was like a bad movie you watch on afternoon TV; you keep asking yourself why you're even watching it. But it had never seemed quite so dumb before, not when it was tucked inside Brad's head where no one else could see it.

Gil's problems kept getting worse. He was shooting more, trying to save the day—and save himself from disgrace. But he couldn't hit anything. Some of the kids in the stands started to boo, and someone yelled, "Take Gil out." Others started to yell at him for being such a gunner and a glory boy. Brad could see Gil's frustration growing. His face was red, maybe from effort, but probably just as much from emotion.

Brad was feeling increasingly uncomfortable. Seeing all this, so real, was painful in a way that he hadn't expected. He wanted it to end; he really wished he could cancel the whole thing somehow. He just didn't like the way it made him feel about himself.

But all was moving along just as Brad had seen it before. Right on schedule, toward the end of the game, the Grandview team fell behind with only seconds remaining on the clock. The coach called time-out.

Then it all started—Brad had seen it so many times. The coach called on Theo, and the crowd went crazy. Out he came. He stripped off his warm-ups, bounced up and down a few times, and nodded as he listened to instructions. Gil was the one the coach told to sit down. He grabbed a towel, dropped into his seat, and covered his face. Maybe he was crying.

Brad watched Gil. He knew what was going to happen in the game. But he had never watched Gil before, not from this point on. Gil really did feel bad, but once the action started, he seemed most concerned about what was happening on the floor.

Theo took the inbound pass. There was a full-court press, but he dribbled between his legs and behind his back, split the two guys guarding him, and got the ball over the ten-second line. He slowed at the top of the key, gave a guy a head fake, and drove the lane. Another guy picked him up, but he faked and pivoted and went to the hoop. The shot was a twisting, underhand lay-up, and the ball spun on the iron a couple of times and then hung a full second before it dropped through. At the same moment the buzzer sounded.

But what else? He was fouled in the act of shooting. There was no time on the clock, so the referee cleared the lane. Little Theo stepped to the line as the crowd hushed on one side and yelled like crazy to distract him on the other. He bounced the ball, eyed the basket. The tension mounted.

But Brad was watching Gil all this time. Gil had jumped up as Theo had driven toward the basket.

He had cheered for Theo when the ball fell through. And now he was waiting anxiously.

Swish. Of course. The home team won. Up on shoulders Theo went, everyone mobbing around him. He grinned, pleading to be let down.

But something was happening—something Brad had never noticed. Gil was one of the guys hoisting Theo in the air. It was strange. How could Brad have missed that every time before?

Brad was edging away by now, getting ready to leave. He had just realized that this was the one where the kids start yelling for Theo to give a speech. The announcer handed Theo the mike and he said, "All I did was come in and do my best. The credit goes to the guys who played the whole game. For me it's a big enough honor just to sit on the bench with such a fine bunch of fellows."

Oh, please. No one would ever come up with a line that bad. "Theo must have made that one up," Brad mumbled to himself. "I don't remember thinking up anything that stupid."

And then Brad saw Kathy coming. She was running across the floor, and she was bending down to throw her arms around Theo, giving him a long kiss —right on the lips. This was no sixth-grader kiss. This was something right out of the movies.

Brad held on for another few seconds, watching until Theo stepped back and said, "Wow." And then he was gone. He didn't want to hear Kathy say the rest: "You're the greatest player I've ever seen.

You're our hero." And then, whispering in his ear: "If you asked me to start going with you right now, I'd say yes."

Brad was running. He was trying to get as far away from that school as he could get. It was all so humiliating. It didn't matter that the kids didn't know who had thought the stuff up—Brad knew. And Kathy had known Brad since kindergarten. She had rarely bothered to say so much as hello to him. The only time she had ever touched him in her life was once when she patted him on the head and said something sarcastic—ending with "nice try, shorty." Brad really didn't want to think about that.

But she was so pretty—the prettiest girl in the school. What were people going to think when she said that stuff to Theo? They had to know something was wrong this time. Kathy just wouldn't, no way, just wouldn't go with that little runt. That was as impossible as Theo doing a slam dunk.

SEVEN:

Brad was lying on his bed, concentrating. He was trying to think Theo into his room. He pictured him sitting on the chair across from his bed, one foot up on the rung, the other hiked over his knee, and leaning back with his hands behind his head. It was what Theo would do, he thought. But Theo didn't show. Just the one in his head—nothing in the chair.

"We need to talk," he finally said out loud. "You absolutely can't do the one about the lion. You just can't. Can you hear me?" Still no Theo, not even a voice.

Brad gave up and turned on the radio. In a few minutes his dad called him down to dinner. "How's the philosopher today?" he asked when Brad came into the kitchen.

"Okay."

But Mom said, "You know Brad, I was thinking some more about that question of yours. I don't know how much you have heard about Sigmund Freud, but he said that—"

"Quick, run," Dad said. "If your mother starts in on Freud, you'll be stuck here all evening."

"George, be quiet," she complained, but she was laughing all the same.

"Please don't start in on all your psychology stuff," Dad said. "I just want to spend a pleasant few minutes with my lovely wife, my fine son, and three or four pork chops."

That was the end of that. Brad was relieved. But the next question was the one Brad had hoped to avoid. "What was the deal with the big basketball game today at school?" Mom asked.

"We had a ball game with Westridge. That's all."

"Who won?" Dad asked. He had just sliced off a huge chunk of margarine and was dropping it on to his baked potato.

"We did."

"You mean Grandview?"

"It was really our recreation-league team."

"You didn't play, did you?"

"No."

"You didn't even try out, as I recall."

"How could I do that? I'm about the shortest kid in the sixth grade."

"Hey, listen, lots of guys who aren't that big play the game. Look at me. When I was your age, I—"

"Hey guys, let's not go over this one again. We've been through it too many times before. If Brad doesn't like sports, that's his own business. We all agreed to that."

Brad watched Dad. He got that disgusted look on his face, rolled his eyes, and then said nothing.

"What I want to know," Mom said, "is who this Theo kid is. Everyone in town is talking about him. He's supposed to be about half your size and the best athlete anyone's ever seen."

"Oh, is that right?" Dad said. He was interested again. "Is he really that good, Brad?"

"Yeah, he's pretty good."

Dad didn't dare say, I told you so, but he gave Brad a significant nod.

"According to Melinda Brimhall, the kid can do anything. He's a whiz at math—and everything else, I guess. They say he knocked a softball clear out of the playground, across the street, and down into the park."

Dad laughed at that. "I think the story must have grown a little."

"Maybe so. But Melinda said Gil is talking about nothing else these days. Why haven't you said anything about him, Brad?"

The question. He had been expecting it. What he didn't have was an answer. "I don't know. I guess I kind of forgot about it."

"He didn't really hit a ball that far, did he?" Dad said.

"Uh . . . I guess he sort of did."

"Sort of?"

"Yeah. Some things . . . you know . . . look better than they are."

"Well, did he hit it that far, or did it only look like it?"

If Dad only knew. "I'd say that it looked like it."

"And so what about the ball? Did it end up down in the park or not?"

"Well, no. He went and got it."

Another eye roll. "But did he hit it there or didn't he?"

"Well . . . I guess he did. In a way."

Dad looked over at his wife. "Eileen, this is your fault. This kid doesn't know when a baseball's hit in the park and when it isn't. He thinks baseballs are hit 'sort of' in the park 'kind of.' "

"Leave him alone," Mom said, laughing. "Great minds see the complexity of life. They don't want simple answers to everything."

"That's right," Brad said, trying to laugh. He had been gulping his food fast, and now he was going to make his exit.

But the doorbell rang. And something told Brad immediately that trouble was waiting on the other side of the front door. He hurried to the door himself, and sure enough, the worst possible case had presented itself. It was Theo.

"Hi Brad. Were you trying to get in touch with me?"

"Yes. But don't come through the door. Leave. And then meet me in my bedroom. Come through the wall or something."

"What? I don't do that. I've never gone through a wall."

"Well, start." But it was too late. Mom was coming down the hall. Brad considered slamming the door quickly, but he knew it wouldn't work. Instead, he said, hurriedly, "Come this way and head straight to my room. Don't say anything."

But Theo hadn't taken three steps before Mom's voice rang down the hall. "Hello there."

"Oh. How do you do? Nice to see you, Mrs. Hill."

Mom walked closer and then said, "I don't believe I've met you. But I'm willing to bet you're the *famous* Theo Zephyr—the kid who can do everything."

"Yes, I'm Theo Zephyr. I can't do everything, but I certainly do some things very well."

Brad could see the surprise in his mother's eyes; she hadn't expected that answer. "I understand you've just moved to town. Where do you live?"

Theo looked thoughtful. Brad could see something strange coming. He hurried to say, "His parents are looking for a place. They may not end up staying in Grandview."

"Oh, really? I wonder if they've looked at the Millers' place. It's for sale."

"I don't know," Brad said. "Theo and I have to talk about something—a school project. See you later." Brad started to walk, but Theo wasn't coming.

"Mrs. Hill," he said. "It's so nice to talk to you. I rarely get a chance to see you. Brad almost never includes you when I'm around."

"But I thought you only moved here a couple of days ago."

"Ah. Is that what Brad said? I think he still thinks about it that way. He has some funny notions about time."

Now Mom really was interested. "Funny notions?"

"Yes. I suppose it's actually reality as much as time. He labels certain things unreal, mental things, for instance, and then, not accepting their existence, he discounts them as though they hadn't occupied time."

Mom nodded, momentarily baffled, and the boys headed up the stairs, but the escape was not quite that easy. "Theo," Mom said, "it just struck me that you must be the one who's been introducing Brad to all the interesting questions he's been asking. Did you tell him that everyone actually knows everything?"

"Yes, yes. I'm glad to know he talked to you about that. Were you able to help him at all?"

"Well, I'm not sure. But I'm curious to know what you meant."

"Oh, I never mean anything."

"Excuse me?"

"Certainly. You're excused."

"No, I mean . . . do you think we can know things but not know that we know them?"

"No, not at all. How could a person ever know a thing? He could see a thing, of course, smell it and taste it and all that, but I don't see how he could know it."

"But didn't you say that we could know everything?"

"Yes. We can know all that is knowable. But there's no use trying to know a thing. It probably wouldn't be worth knowing anyway."

Mom smiled, but Brad could see she was really intrigued. He knew he'd better get Theo away from her before this whole conversation got out of hand. "Mom, we really do need to get started."

"Okay, fine," she said. "But I want to talk to Theo again some time. He's got my curiosity going now. He's quite the little philosopher."

"Oh, I certainly hope not," Theo said, as Brad pushed him on up the stairs. Brad wondered if he was going to have to spend the rest of his life tugging Theo around, getting him out of conversations.

"Theo," Brad said, "please, please, don't tell my parents who you are."

"You mean you haven't told them?"

"No. I'd never do that."

"Strange," Theo said. He walked over and sat down on the chair, and he assumed the exact pose that Brad had imagined.

"Why wouldn't you come when I wanted you? I thought and thought, and you wouldn't appear."

"This isn't a magic show, Brad. Have a little respect."

"If I made you up, I should be able to make you do things."

"No," Theo said, and he sounded almost grave. "I think by now you should know what you know about that. I'm not that much in your control any longer. I haven't been for quite some time."

"Well, you can't do anything I haven't thought of."

The smile returned. "Interesting," Theo said. "Now that you've thought that very thought, I might just be able to—"

"No. Please don't. The lion thing is bad enough. You won't do that one, will you?"

"Of course I will. That's what I do."

"Theo, think about it. We don't have a zoo here. There's no circus in town. Where would a lion come from?"

"Oh Brad, you wear me out sometimes. Those are not my problems. The lion has come into your school hundreds of times. You never made me explain him before. We did almost nothing but the lion there for a while. You never seemed to worry about it then."

Brad knew the time Theo was talking about—during basketball tryouts. The memory hurt. Brad had wanted to go out for basketball more than anything, but there was no way he was going to make the team, and he had known it. So he had claimed he didn't want to play.

"Theo, you've got to give me more of an idea of what I'm supposed to do to stop this whole thing. All this stuff is driving me crazy."

"Why? I thought you liked it."

"Well, I don't anymore. And if people figure out what's going on, I hate to think what they're going to say about me."

"Is that really what's bothering you?"

"Yeah, it is," Brad said, but then he added, "And you know what else. Now that I see all this stuff, it makes me feel like an idiot to know I ever used to sit around and think about it."

"Brad, I can't help that. I didn't create the state of things. You did. But I will say this. Everything in this world is really very simple—except for the things that look simple. They usually aren't."

"Oh brother." Brad sat down on his bed. "You can't blame all this on me, Theo. You're not the one I made up. You've changed a lot more than your name."

"I've grown larger than you expected. That's all."

"But you used to be my friend. You didn't talk this

way to me. You did things with me. We used to play for hours, and you said things I wanted you to say."

"You were little then. You played alone, and you wanted someone. You were wonderful then, Brad. You were a lovely little guy. So was I. We just changed, that's all."

"Do you still like me?"

"You have to answer that one, Brad."

"Why?"

"You know why."

Brad tried to think of what Theo meant. He thought maybe he did understand at least that much. But there was no getting any further. He certainly wasn't in any danger of knowing everything.

"Theo, we're still friends, even with your new name and everything. I've gotten mad at you the last couple of days, but I still like you. I really do. And I think you like me. Friends don't hurt each other. Don't do the lion. Okay?"

"I'm sorry, Brad. I don't have that choice. And you know what else is coming, don't you?"

"I don't want to do that one anymore. I really don't, Theo."

Theo walked over and patted Brad softly on the shoulder. "Brad, all you need to know is hovering right before your eyes right now. Just see it. You're really close. I'll go now. You look through, and in, and around the words we've just said and see what is there."

And then Theo was gone. Just gone.

Brad tried to remember all that they had said, and he made a few stabs at some ideas, but he couldn't really get hold of anything. What he did feel was very uncomfortable, almost frightened by something he couldn't really formulate.

On top of that, he was preoccupied with other worries. Wait until Mom asked about Theo having left without ever having come downstairs. It was going to be another one of those "the baseball was hit sort of in the park kind of" conversations.

EIGHT:

Brad thought up a plan. First, he sneaked down the stairs, checked to see that his parents weren't around, opened the front door, said, "I'll see you, Theo," and shut the door. Second, in the morning, when his mom woke him up, he told her that he didn't feel at all well. He thought he'd better stay home from school.

But Mom was not an easy one to con. She walked over and felt his head. "Brad," she said, with some firmness, "you don't have a fever. You don't have any symptoms. I can't think of any reason why you should—"

"I have a bad headache."

"Then get your fanny out of bed, take an aspirin, and head to school."

"That's what Dad would say. You're supposed to be the one who uses psychology on me." Brad couldn't help smiling.

"I just did. It's the homemade kind. Now get up or you're going to be late."

That was the end of part two of the plan. There was no part three. Brad was in trouble. Maybe he could make up a part three called "run away from home." The trouble with that was that he hated sleeping anywhere but in his own bed. And so, as he walked to school, he told himself, "Okay, let the stupid lion come. Theo's the one who's going to have to explain it all." But that thought wasn't very comforting.

Brad avoided Theo when he got to class. He went straight to his own desk. But Theo came walking over and said, loud enough for everyone in the back of the room to hear, "It's going to be the full one —the one with the parade."

Brad cringed. The version with the parade was the most unbelievable one of all. Theo knew that. And why was he announcing it out loud? He seemed to be trying to make things as embarrassing as he could.

Brad could hardly think, let alone study, but

lunchtime came, and it still hadn't happened. He got a chance to say to Theo at lunch, "I know I can't stop you from doing it, but you don't have to say anything to anyone."

"Like what?"

"You mentioned the parade right in front of a bunch of kids this morning."

"Oh, well, what difference does that make? They'll see it this afternoon."

"But they don't have to know I invented the whole story."

"Oh, they'll know that in time too. There's no escaping that."

"Theo, you can't—"

But someone had come too close, and Brad had to stop. And then, when they went back to class, it all began to happen. First there was the scream. The lion daydream always started that way. Someone screamed, and then the door flew open and Mrs. Bednar, another sixth-grade teacher, stuck her head in the door and yelled, in a voice full of terror. "Clear the building. There's a lion in the school."

It occurred to Brad that this really didn't make any sense. Why didn't they just shut the door and stay put? A lion can't open doors. But it didn't happen that way. Just as always, Mrs. Hardy stood up and said, in a voice full of panic, "Hurry students; run for your lives!"

She would never say that. Why didn't anyone seem to notice that? But it was too late. Everyone was running, and out in the hallway all was chaos. Kids and teachers were running around like they were crazy. All those fire drills over the years, and now, look at how they were acting.

Brad kept hearing screams, and people were bumping into him, coming from all directions, but he just walked straight to the doors that led to a sort of garden area in the middle of the school. It was outdoors, but it was surrounded by the building. He knew that's where Theo would do it. That's where it always happened. The kids would run all around, but most of them, instead of ever heading outside and away from the school, would all come into this area where they could get trapped. It was about as illogical as anything he could think of.

That's where they were all right. And they were all huddled together, clinging to each other, screaming and crying. It had really never looked this stupid before.

Some kid Brad didn't even know grabbed him by the arm. He looked like a third-grader, maybe. He was almost as big as Brad, but he had a baby face. "What are we going to do?" he said, and his eyes were full of terror. If he had been an actor in a movie, the director would have fired him for overacting.

"Don't sweat it," Brad said. "It won't—"

"Oh no, here it comes. What'll we do? What'll we do? Oh, who will save us? Who?"

"Look kid, that's your own material. I didn't make that up."

But the kid was paying no attention. He was pleading for mercy, mumbling something about being too young to die. A lot of other kids were doing the same thing. Did they think this lion spoke English or something?

But on the lion came, a male, with a huge mane and a wild-eyed look. Brad had to admit, the thing was pretty frightening. He found himself taking a few steps back. Everyone else was doing the same thing, and the crush was getting awful, not to mention all the screaming and pleading.

And there was Kathy Noyes, somehow left at the front of the crowd. She had that pretty, blue dress on that Brad liked so much, and a blue ribbon holding her blonde hair back. How in the world had she known to wear that today? The lion paced toward her, then slowed to a stop about twenty feet away. He looked evil and angry, ready to attack. But just then Gil stepped forward. "Get away," he yelled.

Brad had to admit, that was pretty brave. No one else seemed ready even to give it a shot. But the lion let out a tremendous roar, and, as always, Gil dropped to his knees and started to cry. It was a cheap shot; Brad really felt that this time. For a moment he had the compulsion to run up front and face the lion himself, to do that part instead of Theo. And then, after it was all over, he could tell everyone what was really going on. That would at least take some courage. There was something really disgusting about standing back here just watching.

But he didn't step forward, and suddenly Theo was there. Up until now, Brad hadn't even seen the guy. Out he stepped, however, and he said, "Don't worry, Kathy, I'll handle this." One thing about Theo, he had that big, strong voice. He could bring off a line.

Everything got very quiet, the way it always did, and Theo began to take one slow step after another toward the big lion. It took a full minute, at least, before he was standing face to face with the thing—and with Theo's height, it really was face to face.

"I don't fear you," Theo announced. "And you'll harm no one here—especially not this beautiful girl." At least he left out the line Brad had used a couple of times about being in love with her. Maybe Theo did have some mercy.

The lion let out another enormous roar and lunged forward, but Theo didn't move a muscle. The lion stopped short, his great jaws in Theo's face. If the lion had bad breath, Theo would know it.

But Theo gave a little laugh. "That's all you are is noise," Theo said. "You don't scare me one bit. Now settle down and stop bothering these poor, frightened children. They've done nothing to you."

What followed was an intense few moments when the two—man and beast (or at least little kid and beast)—stared into each other's eyes. Brad had always thought of this as the time of searching each other's souls, of testing each other's true grit. And then the lion slowly settled down, like a kitten, dropping its eyes from Theo and curling up as though it wanted to be petted.

Theo took off his belt; he was now moving with ease and confidence. "Here we go, fellow," he said, and he put the belt around the lion's neck. Brad almost wished he had made up a version where Theo's beltless pants fell down, but it was too late for that now. What was really happening was the usual: The kids were silent, awestruck; Theo was supreme but not cocky; Kathy was whispering, "You're the bravest boy I've ever known."

And Brad was whispering, "Oh, gag me," but that wasn't part of the show.

Theo tugged gently at the belt, and the lion got up, and then Theo walked from the school with the lion following meekly behind. Gradually the kids got their voices back: "What a guy." "He saved our lives." "He may be little, but nothing scares him." "He's the greatest hero this town has ever known."

Brad was just glad it was over. But no such luck. This was the one where the newspaper reporters were suddenly arriving from all over the world. Evening papers in every nation of the world would be headlined, "Small Boy Tames Lion," or "Utah Boy Saves Thousands of Lives." Thousands? That's what they said.

The whole afternoon was crazy. School was let out, and then, suddenly, a parade was somehow organized. Kids from the school hurried over to Main Street, and lots of people from around town were showing up. Brad was in a kind of daze, but he walked over too and watched it all go by.

First there were two flag bearers carrying a banner that read: THEO ZEPHYR: HERO OF GRANDVIEW. Next came the high-school band in full uniform. And then, there was Theo sitting in the back of a bright red convertible. Brad had held out some hope that he might be alone, but no such luck. Kathy was right up there next to him, looking gorgeous and leaning all over Theo. Somehow a float, complete with a papier mâché Theo and lion, had come into existence, and it was trailing after Theo. A sign on it proclaimed: HE FACED THE LION AND SAVED OUR LIVES.

The parade moved slowly toward the old courthouse building, and a huge crowd followed along. Half the town was there by now. Theo was led from the car to a platform that had appeared, nicely constructed on the steps of the courthouse and all decorated with patriotic bunting. A banner was strung across the second floor of the courthouse: THANK YOU, THEO ZEPHYR.

"I don't remember that one," Brad told himself. "I think Theo is making some of this stuff up."

The mayor walked with Theo to the front of the platform, and the crowd went crazy, cheering wildly for at least five minutes. Brad couldn't believe it. He saw Mrs. Nelson, from his neighborhood; she was actually sobbing, tears dripping from her cheeks. And Fred Clayson, the guy who owned the bank in town, was shouting, "What a kid! What a tremendous kid!" Theo was pouring it on too thick; it had never been quite this extreme before.

Finally, the mayor, Irwin Rohatinsky, (who was actually the former mayor, but no one seemed to notice) got the crowd to quiet, and he gave his speech. "Ladies and gentlemen, friends and neighbors, and especially the fortunate children of our Grandview Elementary School—I'm here today to praise the finest young man this community has ever known, perhaps the most courageous boy in the entire world. Like David of old, our own little Theo has stood in the face of danger and saved us all."

How many people could one lion eat? Come on, mayor.

But the speech went on and on, and then Theo received a beautiful gold medal on a red, white, and blue ribbon. This was placed around his neck by none other than Kathy Noyes, who, right in front of the whole town, planted another big kiss on Theo's lips. The girl had no shame.

Brad stood at the back of the crowd, watching, shaking his head. Somehow, he felt this had to be the end. Everyone was going to wake up the next morning and say, "Wait a minute. We've been conned."

The mayor marched Theo back to the convertible for some more parading. Brad half expected sky-scrapers to start appearing so that the people in town would have a place to throw ticker tape from.

Brad decided it was time to get away. He walked home very slowly, avoiding anyone he knew. He really had to think, to try to understand what he was feeling. It was rotten of Theo to make all this stuff happen right out in front of everyone in the real world. He had felt that all along. But now he was not at all sure what the real world was. Maybe Theo was right. Maybe there was no difference between the things he had always called real and the ones he had thought were just made up.

NINE:

Brad went straight to his room when he got home. For a time he just sat there, still trying to believe that all this had really happened, but gradually he couldn't keep his thoughts from turning to the next day. He knew he had to figure some things out. Up until now this had all been crazy, but if Theo did the one he called the "big one," that was another matter. Brad simply had to stop it.

He really was finding some things out about himself, or at least he had been experiencing some new feelings that he was trying to understand, but he had no idea whether he now "knew what he knew." If only Theo would talk straight.

After a little while, Mom came upstairs. He could see something was on her mind. "Brad, I was just coming home and listening to the car radio. I heard on the news about this lion business. Did all that really happen?"

Brad nodded. He was sitting on his bed, but now he lay back, trying to look relaxed. "Yeah. I guess so."

"You guess so?"

"Well, I mean, I don't know what they said about it on the radio."

"A lion supposedly came into your school, and Theo walked up to him and put his belt around its neck and led it away."

"Yeah. That was about it."

She was staring at him. He could see the wheels turning. Maybe she wasn't buying it. "Brad, how can you just sit there and answer like that? You act like this sort of thing happens every day."

Almost, he thought, but that's not what he said. "Well, it happened a few hours ago. I guess I'm not as excited as I was then."

She hesitated, looking skeptical. "Did you go to the parade?"

"Yeah."

"And Mayor Mecham gave Theo a medal?"

"Well, actually, it was the old mayor. But yeah, he gave him a medal."

"Where did that come from?"

"The medal?"

"Yes."

"I don't know."

"I don't either." She was studying him very closely. Brad tried to act as though nothing were out of the ordinary. The two kept watching each other —it was the lion and Theo scene all over again. But it was Brad who looked away finally, and it was Mom who said, "Brad, something very strange is going on around here."

Brad tried to shrug, casually. He didn't dare try his voice. She would hear his tenseness.

"Where did the lion come from? Has anyone figured that out yet?"

"I don't know."

"Brad, I've been asking a few people about the Zephyrs. No one seems to have met Theo's parents. You told me they were looking for a house, but I talked to Elizabeth Harrison, and she hasn't even heard of them. Her real-estate company is the only one in town. I saw Teresa Ridd today. Her house is up for sale, so I asked her whether the Zephyrs had contacted her. She's never heard of them either. Margie Hunter, at the bank; Tom McGarry at the grocery store; Emory Shaw, who knows everyone in town—not one of them has heard of this family. Brad, this town isn't very big. You can't be around here for several days and not have anyone know about it."

Brad didn't reply. He didn't look at her. "Have you met his parents?"

"No."

Brad glanced up. Mom had her hands on her hips, and she was drilling him with those sharp eyes. "Listen Brad, I don't get this. I really don't. For three days now you've been acting just plain odd. And things have been happening that simply can't be explained. I talked to Sherm Wells, my friend who teaches physics at the college, and he said there is no human way that a kid four feet tall could slam dunk a basketball. Absolutely no way. He said it must be a story the kids have made up. Is it?"

"I don't know, Mom. Why are you getting after *me?*"

"I'm not getting after you. I'm just . . . worried, I guess. When things happen that I don't understand, I get concerned. Especially when they seem to be having some sort of strange effect on my son."

"I'm okay."

She was waiting him out. When he finally looked up again, she was watching his eyes, as though she were trying to find something there. "Tell me this: Did you see Theo make that basket?"

"Uh . . . yeah."

"Was it a slam dunk? I mean, did he literally jump all the way up and slam the ball through the net from above the rim?"

"I think so."

"Oh Brad, come on. What is this? You haven't

answered a question straight since this Theo kid came to town. Now look at me. There's something going on, isn't there? Something strange?" Brad looked at her, but he didn't answer. "Why don't you want to talk to me about it?"

Brad took a long breath, and then he got up the courage to say, "I just don't. Not yet."

"But you do admit that something strange has been happening?"

"Yes."

"Can you tell me honestly that there's nothing for me to worry about?"

"Yeah. I'm sort of mixed up, but that's all."

"This is not easy for me, Brad. I want to force you to tell me. But it runs against my grain to do that. I can't let this go on much longer though."

"It's nothing all that serious, Mom. It's just weird."

"Okay. I guess I'll have to take your word for that."

But she wasn't leaving. Brad waited for a very long time before he looked back up at her. She was thinking now, not watching him so closely. She came over and sat down on the bed. "Brad, I've decided to ask you something that you might think is really odd. I probably shouldn't, but . . . well, anyway, I'm going to ask."

Brad really didn't need this. He knew she was getting close to something.

"When you were little, you had an imaginary

friend. You used to play with him. Do you remember that?"

"Sure."

"Tell me about him."

"Why?"

"Just tell me what you remember about him."

"I don't know. He was little, and he would play with me when I didn't have anyone else to play with, since I didn't have any brothers or sisters."

"And what did he do?"

"What do you mean?"

"It seems to me that he used to do things that other kids couldn't do. You used to tell me all sorts of wild stories about him. He could jump over trees and run faster than anyone—all sorts of things like that. Isn't that right?"

"Yeah." Brad turned a little and looked toward the wall.

"One time you told me that a lion came into your room, and your friend faced him and wasn't afraid. And then it seems to me you told me he took off his belt and put it around the lion's neck and led it out of the house. That was a long time ago, but that's what I remember. Today, when I heard that radio account, it all came back to me."

She hesitated, as though she wanted Brad to say something. Brad did want to. In fact, he didn't know why he was resisting anymore. If he told her, maybe she could help him figure out what to do. All the same, something in him held back.

"Doesn't it strike you as odd that you would think up something like that years and years ago, and then something so similar would happen at your school today?"

"Yeah." And then he added, trying to make his voice natural, "It is kind of weird."

"That's all you have to say?"

Brad nodded.

"Oh Brad, this is driving me crazy. What did that friend of yours look like?"

"He was little."

"I know, but I remember you told me other things about him. He had big ears and messy hair. Didn't you get him from TV or something like that?"

"I saw a kid in a commercial. It was just a little cartoon thing. But I told you that was what my friend looked like. After that, I always pictured him that way." This was only coming back to Brad now.

"You don't ever think about him now, do you?"

"Sometimes I do."

"But you don't make up stories and pretend you're talking to him and things like that?"

"I'm too old for that now." That was true. It is what he believed.

"What was his name?"

For some reason, this above all else, he didn't want to say. He just wouldn't. "I don't remember."

The doorbell rang downstairs, and Brad was glad of it. He started to get up. "Wasn't it Bradley? Didn't you call him by your own name?"

Brad was trying to get out of the room.

"Your dad started calling you Buddy, and that's what we always called you in those days. It seemed so strange to me that you would make up a friend and give him your own name, while we were calling you something else."

Brad slipped past his mother and headed for the stairs. He was angry. She didn't have to keep doing this. Downstairs, he pulled the door open—and there was Theo. Brad was so stunned he couldn't think of anything to say.

But Theo came right in and started up the stairs. "Come on, Brad. We need to talk about a few things before we do the big one."

And there was Mom at the top of the stairs. "Theo," she said, "I've been hearing some amazing things about you." She was calculating, not just making conversation. Brad could hear it in her voice. She was going to try to pin Theo down.

"Yes. That's what I do mostly. Amazing things."

"You actually stared down a lion?"

"Yes. That's a good one, isn't it? The kids loved it."

"How can you do such things?"

"Ask Brad. He knows more about it than I do."

Brad was trying to get past his mom, but she was holding her own this time.

"Theo, who are you? There's something strange going on."

"Yes. I'm sure it seems that way. I'm Theo

Zephyr. I'm who I am. I've never had any other answer to your question. But I do know why you ask. I'm not offended."

"Why can you jump higher than other kids?"

"I have no way of knowing. Brad knows that."

Mom looked over at Brad. He shrugged and shook his head.

"He tells me he doesn't know. I've been quizzing him about you—and he won't say much of anything."

"Mrs. Hill, I can only say what I've said. I have no other words for your question. But I will say this: I like you very much."

That one got her. She really couldn't think of her next question, and the boys got on by to Brad's bedroom. Inside the room, Theo said, "Well, what about it? Did you enjoy it?"

"That parade and everything? No. It was stupid."

"Yes, of course. Is that all you have to say?"

"No. I'm asking you not to do the other one—the one with Gil. I don't like that one anymore. I don't want you to do it."

"What do you know? Can you tell me yet?"

"Okay. I've been thinking. And this is what I want to tell you. I always say I'm not jealous of Gil. But I am. I really do wish I was good at sports, and I wish I did as well in school. I've been jealous of him since clear back in first grade."

"Yes, of course. What else?"

"I don't know what else."

"Fine. We'll go ahead with it then. Maybe we can do it first thing in the morning and get it over with."

"Wait. Don't disappear."

"Why not?"

"I really do want to stop this whole thing right now. But you have to help me understand."

"Brad, by now you should be seeing more. You're still thinking of 'everything' as the capital of Delaware and all that sort of thing. You're looking for facts. Nothing is so unreal as a fact."

"Theo, how can it not be real if it's a fact?"

"Brad, I want you to stop this. I don't think you're really trying. You insist on looking at the surface— at *things*. I'm real. You have to know *me*. That's how you can stop this whole thing."

"Can I have some time to think about that?"

"Time has nothing to do with it, Brad. Just see what is."

And then Theo was gone.

TEN:

Brad tried harder than ever before, but he really didn't know what Theo wanted him to know. He tried to think through everything that had happened since Theo had arrived, all the things Theo had said. He knew he was changed in some ways, that he felt quite different about himself, but he didn't know what he had learned from it all.

The one thing that kept coming to mind was that he'd better warn Gil. He was not likely to be able to stop Theo from going through with the next one, so he'd better at least let Gil know what was going to happen. So he headed downstairs. But he had forgotten about his mother. She was waiting in the living room, where she could see the front door.

"Where are you going, Brad?" she said.

Brad hadn't seen her at first. He spun around. "Uh, I just thought I'd go over to Gil's for a minute."

"Gil Brimhall?"

"Yeah."

"That's something new. Are you guys getting to be friends?"

"Yeah, I guess."

"What about Theo? Isn't he going with you?"

"Oh, he left a few minutes ago."

Mom got up. She had that look again. "Brad, I've been sitting right here since I left your room. I've been waiting to talk to Theo. There's no way he could have come down those stairs without my seeing him."

"Maybe he jumped out my window. You know how he can jump."

"Yes. Over trees, for example."

Brad tried to smile. "I'll be back in a little while." He headed out the door. Mom was definitely on to this thing. He could see that she was struggling to decide whether she really believed what she believed. Brad knew exactly how she felt.

But for the moment, there was something a lot more important that he had to take care of. Gil lived about three blocks away. For some reason, Brad found himself running all the way. When he got to Gil's he started up the walk to the front door, but then he heard some voices around back. He figured it must be Gil and some of the guys.

Brad walked around to the back. Gil was playing catch with Phil and a couple of other guys—Elmo Benson and Mike Hindmarsh. They were all on a summer-league team together. "Hi you guys," Brad said, and all four looked over. Brad could see that all of them were surprised, especially Gil.

"Hello Brad," Gil said with no enthusiasm. "What are you doing?"

"I was just . . . actually, I wanted to talk to you, Gil." Brad was still a little out of breath, and he was nervous.

"Okay."

"I mean . . . alone." This was really embarrassing. Gil looked at him like he was some sort of weirdo, and Phil and Elmo started to laugh.

"So what's the big deal?" Gil said.

"Could you walk around in front for a minute? It's something quite important."

"Where's your little buddy Theo? I thought you two would be hanging around together from now on."

Brad could feel Gil's anger. He really didn't blame him. "If I could just talk to you for about two minutes, that's all I—"

"Okay, okay."

Gil tossed the baseball over to Phil, and then he walked over to the gate where Brad was standing. He opened it and walked through, tucking his baseball glove under his arm. When they got to the front lawn he turned around and stuck his fingers into his jeans pockets. "Okay, what do you want?"

"Gil, this is going to sound strange, but you're just going to have to trust me. I know what I'm talking about."

Gil looked skeptical, but when Brad didn't go on, he finally said, "Okay. What?"

"If I were you, I'd stay home from school tomorrow. Just tell your mom that you're sick or something. If you come to school, I'm pretty sure something bad is going to happen to you."

Gil seemed to see that Brad meant what he said, but he clearly didn't like it. "Look Brad, I don't know what you're talking about, but it must have something to do with Theo."

"Yes, it does. But that's all I can say."

Gil was thinking things over, but the muscles in his cheeks were tightening. Brad had known him for a long time; that look always meant he was getting mad. "What more could Theo do to me?"

"He hasn't done anything yet. Not to you."

"Oh, sure. This has only been the worst week of my life, since that little jerk got here."

It was true. And Gil was right. Theo was behind it all. But that's not what Brad said. "Look, that lion would have scared anyone."

That was the wrong thing to say. "Hey, I didn't see you out there trying to do anything. I tried to scare the stupid thing away."

"I know. That took a lot of guts."

Brad knew what Gil was thinking. He had cried in front of everyone. But what he said was, "Theo was just trying to make me look bad."

"I know. That is what happened. He's been doing that all week—in sports and everything. But tomorrow's going to be worse."

"How do *you* know? Is that what he said?"

"Not exactly. But I know."

Gil was watching Brad now. It was almost the way Brad's mom had studied him earlier. Finally he said, "Brad, there's some really screwy stuff going on, and I don't get it."

"I know."

"What do you mean, you know?"

"I think things have been strange this week too."

"I think you do more than *think* so. I think you're in on it. You knew Theo before he came, and he knew you. Every single thing that has happened this week has been all planned out to make me look stupid."

"Not exactly, Gil. I mean, I didn't plan any of it." Brad knew that wasn't exactly true, but he couldn't think what else to say without explaining all kinds of things.

"Look Brad, I don't get what's going on. I don't see how a guy the size of Theo can do all that stuff, and I don't know how he can talk the principal into having a basketball game with another school, or where he got those uniforms. It's all too weird, Brad; it doesn't make any sense. And everything that happens seems to get me messed up more than anyone else. It all sort of seems to be planned out that way."

"Gil, I didn't want any of that stuff to happen. I don't know how Theo does it either."

Gil was getting angrier as he talked, as though the thought of all the embarrassment was building up in him. "But you're in on it, Brad. I know that. Somehow you're helping him."

"How could I do that, Gil? I can't make you have a bad basketball game. You just didn't play as well as you usually do." That wasn't really true either; Brad knew that. It was true in one reality, just not in the other one.

But the answer only frustrated Gil. "Hey, look, I know that. But I knew you were up there loving it. You're not good at any sports—not a single one. But you love to see me do badly, don't you? You always have. You used to treat me like a friend until you started to see that I could beat you at things—and then you turned on me."

That was true. Brad didn't even deny it. A week before, he couldn't have admitted that to himself. "Okay. Okay. But all that doesn't matter right now. You've just got to believe me about something. If you go to school tomorrow, you could get hurt."

"So is that the next plan? Theo's going to try to beat me up?"

"It's not a plan, but it could happen."

"How do you know—unless you two have been talking about it? Look Brad, I know how much you hate me. You'd do anything to mess me up. I think you and Theo are trying to set up something to make me look bad again. You probably want to tell everyone at school that I stayed home because I was afraid of Theo."

Brad decided not to respond to that. He tried to think what he could say to explain. "Look, you said yourself, weird things are happening. But I don't want them to keep happening. I want them to stop. I'm going to try to figure out how to do that, but I've got to get some time to think. If you come to school in the morning, something bad might happen before I can figure out how to stop it."

"Hey, if you think I'm scared of little Theo, forget it. So just tell him to stay away from me, or I'll knock his little head off."

"But you can't, Gil. There's no way. You know how Theo is."

Phil and Elmo came around the corner of the house at about that time. "Come on Gil," Phil said. "What's going on?"

Gil seemed to respond to the new audience. He had always been that way. He actually wasn't such a bad guy to be around most of the time, but some of his friends could bring out the worst in him. It was in front of them that he got cocky, pushy, and even brutal at times. "I'll tell you what," he said, "why don't you fight your own battles for once? Why don't you fight me—without your buddy Theo to help?"

"I don't want to fight you, Gil."

"I'm sure you don't," Phil said, and he laughed.

"Hey Brad," Gil said, "I've given you plenty of chances. You just don't have the guts. You're great at calling names, but you don't dare back it up."

They both knew what this meant. Brad suddenly felt the old anger return. It was the worst memory of Brad's life. The two of them had quarreled at recess, back in the fourth grade, and Brad had gotten mad and called Gil a jerk. Gil had knocked Brad down, and then he had stood over him taunting him, daring him to get up and fight.

But Brad hadn't gotten up, hadn't dared to fight him, and in frustration more than fear, tears had begun to roll down his cheeks. All the guys had laughed. They were all on Gil's side, and for weeks after, they had brought it up. "Is little Bradley afraid? Is he going to start to cry again? He knows how to call people names, but he won't fight it out, will he?" And that's when Brad had started to daydream about getting up, facing Gil, taking him on. That's when all this had started—the "big one," as Theo called it.

But now it really did have to stop. Theo was much

too powerful. If he did the whole thing, pounded and pounded the way . . . the image was too awful. "Gil, I don't want to fight you." He said this softly; he was trying to get his own feelings under control.

But the other boys started laughing, and Gil gave Brad a little push. "You make me sick," he said. "You hate my guts. But you just sit around and hope I'll do something wrong. You never try to beat me. You don't even try in school anymore since you found out I was smarter than you are."

"Lay off, Gil."

But Gil pushed him again, right in the chest. "Why don't you just once stand up to me?" Another push. "Go ahead. Take the first swing. I'll give you a clear shot." He dropped his hands and stuck his jaw out.

"Gil, I don't want to hit you. I came over here to warn you. I just—"

This angered Gil all the more. He gave Brad a harder push, and Brad stumbled backward and fell. "*Warn* me, huh? Are you going to get your little buddy to beat up on me? Well, you tell him I'll fight both of you. You're both such little wimps, I could probably take you on at the same time. Of course, I don't have to worry about you, because you'd break down and cry."

"Okay," Brad said, and now he didn't care. He got up. For an instant he considered charging Gil, slamming into him. But he didn't want to do that.

He didn't ask himself why. "Okay. Just come to school in the morning. And don't tell me I didn't warn you."

Theo was going to get him. And for the moment Brad thought he was going to enjoy it.

ELEVEN :

Brad went home. He told himself he didn't care. He had done all he could do. He had tried to warn Gil; he couldn't help it if Gil wouldn't listen. He had also tried to stop Theo, but Theo wouldn't listen either. Everything was now out of Brad's hands. Gil could just take what was coming to him.

But when Brad went down to dinner, his parents were in a hot debate. "Eileen, that's the craziest story I've ever heard," Dad was saying. "You might as well tell me that the house is full of ghosts and gremlins, or that—"

"Never mind. We'll talk about it later."

Brad slipped into his seat at the table, across from his mother. She looked upset, worried. She looked at Brad and tried to smile, but she didn't come up with much.

"No Eileen, I think we should talk about it now. I think Brad should hear this." He waited but got no agreement, so he leaned one elbow on the table and looked at Brad. He was still wearing a white shirt, from work, but his sleeves were rolled up and his tie was off. "Brad, your mother thinks that your daydreams are turning into . . . real things. Or something of that sort. She—"

"I didn't say that, George."

"You didn't?" Dad twisted back the other way and faced his wife.

"No. I just said that certain coincidences are happening that go beyond ordinary possibilities. And a small boy is doing things not humanly possible. I don't know how to explain it all. I just think . . . well, I don't know what to think."

Dad sat back in his chair and grinned. "My son doesn't know when a baseball lands in the park and when it doesn't. My wife thinks daydreams are sort of possibly maybe turning into kind of, just barely real things. I'm living in the middle of a funny farm here."

But Mom was not about to let him laugh all this off. "George, I don't think this is funny. I'm very concerned. I've never seen Brad act . . . the way he has the last few days."

Dad nodded, as if to say, "All right. I'll play along with you." Again he turned back to Brad; again he put his elbow on the table. "Brad, are you acting strange?"

"Sort of, I guess."

"Now there's a good answer, Eileen. Your son *guesses* that he is acting strange, *sort of.* Maybe he would like to tell us just why he is sort of guessing that he is sort of acting sort of strange."

But Mom saved Brad from having to say anything. "Listen George, Brad and I have talked about this, and I have promised him that I won't probe right now. He feels that he doesn't want to explain at the present time, and I respect his right to do that."

Dad rolled his eyes, and then he stared off at the distant wall for a time. Finally he said, "Then why did we ever start this conversation?"

"I wanted to know what you thought about it. That was my mistake, obviously."

"No, no. Not at all. I'll tell you what I think." He stopped, apparently to bring his thoughts together. But the smile was returning.

"George, never mind. This isn't funny to me."

"Nor to me either. This is a very serious matter. That's why I'm taking it seriously." He was back to a big grin. "First of all, a small boy hits a ball across the street, and he slam dunks a basketball. Or so we hear. But the report comes from a group of children who, like my son, sort of saw it happen kind of."

Brad got himself some lasagne. He was staying out of this if at all possible.

"That's not true," Mom said. "I called Julie Hardy, Brad's teacher. She said Theo hit the ball practically out of sight. She was astounded. And she said that he can do math problems faster than she can give him the numbers."

"All right. Let's deal with those two points. First of all, a baseball bat has what's called a 'sweet spot.' It's the perfect place to produce a long hit. The ball was pitched, and Theo swung his hardest and just happened to really get the good wood on it, as baseball players say. He hit it over the fence. That's impressive, but it's hardly a miracle. I suspect it bounced and rolled into the park. I suspect old lady Hardy knows very little about—"

"She's a young woman, George."

"All right. But she probably knows absolutely zip about baseball, and she probably wasn't even looking when the ball was hit. The whole thing just got blown out of proportion. Someone said the ball got to the park on the fly, and everyone started saying it. You know how kids are."

"What about the slam dunk? Dr. Wells told me there was no way a kid that tall could dunk a basketball."

"There's your answer. He didn't."

"Not according to the boys who were there. Several boys saw it—and one of them was Brad."

Brad was working on his salad. He kept his head down.

"If you think I'm going to ask Brad whether he

kind of saw a slam dunk, more or less, you're nuts, Eileen. Theo didn't make any slam dunk. It's another one of those exaggerations."

"You have all the answers, don't you?"

"Well, I don't know, Eileen. But my answers make a whole lot more sense than your theory. I suspect I'm not the only person in the world who might think your version—the 'magical appearance from the never-never land of a dreamworld'—is stretching it just a bit. I think I could buy the planet Krypton theory ahead of that one."

Mom gave up for a moment and didn't respond. Dad chuckled and then reached for the lasagne. "Look honey," he said in midreach, "I'm just teasing you, but don't you really—"

"Explain the lion. Explain the parade and the banners and the medal. George, if you want to talk about never-never land, just look at that whole event. It could never happen."

Dad looked over at Brad and gave him a wink. "I think," he said, and he shot a little smile at his wife, "that the fact that it *did* happen should enter into our discussion at this point. I know that may seem an unfair demand, but I'm simple-minded about such things."

"No, not simple minded. You want it both ways. When Theo hits the ball out of sight, you just say it didn't happen. But when something too strange to be true does happen, you resort to, 'Well, it happened because it happened.'"

Dad had taken the chance to stuff his mouth with lasagne, and he was still chewing. But he soon swallowed forcefully, and then said, "Ah. That I can explain. The first didn't happen. The second did. That's why I used two different explanations. Do you see how that works?"

"George, where did the lion come from, and by the way, where is it now?"

"Well, I haven't checked into either question. But since the lion wandered into the school, it must have come from somewhere. How's that?"

"There are no lions around here."

"There's one. Maybe it was someone's pet. Maybe it wandered in from California. That's where most weird things come from. I don't know. But it apparently really happened, although the business about staring it down was surely exaggerated. What I suspect is that the thing was as tame as a house cat."

"How did Theo know that?"

"He's the brightest kid around here. We've already established that. He's a genius at math, according to Mrs. Hardy. He just had enough brains to watch the thing and see that it was more scared than dangerous, and he walked over and put his belt on the poor thing and took it outside where all good lions belong."

"George, have you ever talked to Theo? He's like no kid you'll ever meet. His mind just doesn't work the way a kid's mind normally works."

"That's just more proof that he's a genius. I've never met a really bright guy yet who could fit a wrench to a bolt. He would probably be a lot better off if he could cut his IQ in half and make two normal kids."

Dad liked that one. He had settled everything. He began munching his food again, glancing playfully at his wife from time to time. Brad knew that he loved to tease her this way, but he also knew that Mom was not taking it the way she usually did.

"Okay George," she finally said. "You simply don't want to think about this whole situation. Everyone else in town is doing the same thing. I've been asking who organized the parade and made the banners—and a float, for crying out loud. Somehow, things happened far faster than they could have, and every time I ask people about it, they give me the same answer you do: It happened, so it happened."

Dad seemed to sense that he had better lay off. His tone suddenly changed. "Well, there have been some strange things. I'll admit that. But Eileen, I know darn well that if you looked into it more thoroughly there would be an explanation for everything. There has to be."

"Why? How do you know that?"

"Because everything can be explained. That's how. What is, is. I can't think any other way. I'm sorry."

Mom looked at Brad, and now she was watching

for something again. Dad was making her look silly, and only Brad could give her any support for her point of view. But Brad didn't want to get into the same trap she had been squirming around in.

Dad seemed to notice what was happening. "Okay Brad," he said, "can you tell us anything that might explain what's going on?"

"Not really."

"Oh, come on Brad. Lay off all the vague answers. If you know something, tell us."

"George, I told you that he has a right—"

"Eileen, I'm not trying to rob him of his civil rights, for crying out loud. I just asked him whether he could tell us anything to help us understand what's been happening."

Brad had been thinking all along of what he would say if it came to this, but he had never decided. Now he was on the spot. "Well, I think . . . that facts don't make sense a lot of times. If you think about it, we put too much trust in things that are supposed to be real."

"Brad, what is that supposed to mean?"

"Well . . . you know how scientists work and work to explain something, and whatever they discover gets into our textbooks. And then maybe later it turns out it isn't even true."

Now Dad put both elbows on the table, and he leaned forward and put his head in his hands. "Brad, maybe Theo is Superman or the Sugar Plum Fairy or the physical manifestation of your daydreams. Maybe that does make sense. It certainly makes as much sense as this babbling you're doing right now."

"George, that's not fair," Mom said. "Everything he just said is true."

"Of course it is. Science is always continuing its research. That's hardly a shocking thing to realize. But are we supposed to throw out everything we know because of that?"

"No," Brad said. "But we shouldn't take 'facts' too seriously. We'll never understand all that much about the world. Everything we know is just surface stuff. There are things that are more real than facts."

"And what are those things?"

Brad had used up all Theo's material now. He had no answer. But he thought he understood what he had said. It seemed to come clear as he said it.

"Brad, would you kindly tell me what all this has to do with the conversation your mother and I have just been having?"

"It has everything to do with it."

"And would you explain that?"

"I can't. I still don't know. I just know that Mom's right. That stuff with the lion couldn't have happened. And I know you're right. It did. And I know Theo's right. There's something a lot more important than reality."

"Which is?"

"I don't know. That's what I haven't figured out."

Dad let out an enormous moan, and then he dropped his head to his plate, plunging his face into his lasagne, which squished up around his heavy cheeks. He didn't move, but just left his face stuck in the mess.

Brad couldn't help laughing. Mom said, "That's not funny, George," but she was shaking her head and maybe smiling a little.

TWELVE :

In the morning Brad got to school a little early. He hadn't slept very well. He was no longer mad at Gil. He had made up his mind that he was going to do everything he could to get between Theo and Gil and stop them from fighting.

He really wasn't sure exactly what to expect from Theo. He waited outside and watched for him to show up. But it was Gil who came walking up to him, with Phil and Elmo and a couple of other guys. That was the very worst thing that could happen. Brad thought he could possibly get somewhere talking to Gil, but he would have no luck with these other guys around.

"Okay Brad," Gil said, "I'm ready when you are." Brad glanced around. He wondered where Theo was. "He's looking for his little bodyguard," Phil said. "He doesn't dare fight you himself."

"I never said I was going to fight you," Brad said. "I just said to be careful, that something might happen."

"Big talk. Big talk," one of the guys said. "But that's all he does is talk."

Phil stepped up close to Brad, but he spoke to Gil. "Don't let him get away with it this time, Gil. Make him fight you."

Gil seemed to hesitate for a moment, as though he wasn't sure what he wanted to do.

"Get him," Elmo said.

Gil reached out then and gave Brad a shove, the same as he had the night before. "Let's go down to the end of the school where no teachers will come by and break it up. Let's see if you have any guts or not."

Brad had made up his mind never to do that, but now he was tempted to forget all that. He didn't care if he got pounded; at least the guys couldn't say he was afraid.

Another push in the chest. "If you don't fight me now, we'll all know what you are forever." Gil glanced at the other guys, and nodded as if to say, But we already know.

"Look Gil—"

"Go ahead, Brad. I think you should do it yourself this time." Brad recognized the voice and spun around. It was Theo. He had walked up—or appeared—and he was standing there with his hands in his pockets, grinning at Brad. "Go ahead. You do it. It's only fair. I shouldn't get all the fun."

"I don't want to, Theo." Brad was remembering. He saw Gil down and pleading, and he saw the fist smashing into Gil's face over and over again. He saw all the blood.

"Of course you do. You've wanted to for years. You've practically worn me out doing it for you."

"I know. But not for real. Not like this."

"Don't start splitting realities on me again, Brad. Surely you've seen beyond that by now. Just go ahead and do it. Go down to the end of the school with him. You'll know exactly what to do."

"All right," Phil said with enthusiasm, and he grabbed Brad by the shoulder. "Oh, this is going to be good. Come on."

All Gil's friends joined in the strange joy. Mike grabbed Brad by the other arm and helped pull him along. "Come on," he said, sounding pleased with himself. "This time you're not backing out."

But Brad glanced over at Gil and then took another look. He had seen something there for a moment—something in his eyes. It was the last thing he had expected. He tried to think of what it meant as he was moved along by the other boys.

They turned the corner of the school, and then everyone came to a stop. Gil stepped up close. "All right, little Bradley, Theo says you like to think you can beat me up. You take the first punch. You start it, because I'm going to finish it." This got a little cheer from the guys.

Theo said, "Go ahead, Brad. It's your chance. You can have what you want."

"Theo, I don't want it anymore. I don't want to hurt him anymore. When I'm mad I think I do, but. . . ."

All the guys were cracking up. "He doesn't want to hurt you, Gil. He wants to show you some mercy."

Now Gil was laughing, but that look was still there —the one Brad had seen before. Gil jabbed at Brad again. "I'll give you two choices. Hit me or cry. That's how you saved yourself last time."

"Don't start that," Brad said, and he felt the anger rising again. "If you push me too far, you'll wish you hadn't."

All the guys hooted and laughed. "This is it," Mike said. "Little Bradley's going to rip you apart."

Gil's hand shot out again, knocking Brad backward. Brad caught his balance and took a breath. He glanced over at Theo. "I don't want this," he said.

"I'll say you don't, you little pansy." Gil pushed again. "Let's see you cry."

Suddenly Brad drove both hands into Gil's chest, catching him by surprise and knocking him backward. "You cry, Gil. Cry the way you did the other day for everyone. Cry now or you'll wish you had." He stepped up nose to nose with Gil.

"Just take the first swing," Gil said. "I don't want anyone to think I'm going around beating up little kids. But if you take one swing at me, I'll flatten your face."

"Just go ahead," Theo said.

But Theo's calm voice was terrifying. He had arranged this, calculated it. Brad knew it was some sort of test—and he didn't want to fail. "No Theo," he said, stepping back. "I don't feel right about it."

"Tell me what you know then."

"I just hate him because he's bigger than I am—and because he's better at everything. And I hate him because he made me look so stupid in front of everyone. But I am afraid of him."

The other boys, especially Gil, seemed taken off guard by this conversation. They listened and glanced around at each other, but the taunting stopped for the moment.

"Yes, of course," Theo said, sounding impatient. "That's all true—in a way. But it's still a distortion. You know what's really true, Brad."

"No I don't. That's all I know."

"You haven't looked closely enough. You aren't really seeing yet. Go ahead. Pound him now. Drive your fist into his nose and mouth, the way you like to see me do. Don't let the blood bother you; it never has before."

Gil was still listening, with his fists doubled up, but he didn't look as angry as before. The strange confidence in Theo's voice—and the strange things he was saying—must have given him cause to wonder what was going on. But it was Phil who wouldn't let things drop so easily.

"That's right, Brad. You bloody him up. Go ahead and try."

Brad was looking at Gil. "Listen, after that time you did that to me back in fourth grade, I—"

"I didn't do anything to you. You started crying, so I let you go."

"I know, but everyone . . . you know what happened."

"Yeah, I know exactly what happened. You started walking back into school, and those girls started laughing at you. Dawna Anderson and Kathy Noyes and—"

"Shut up."

"Why should I?"

"Look, I—"

"You know what they said to you. 'Do you want my hanky, little Bradley? Does little Bradley need to wipe away his tears?' "

Suddenly Brad charged and bulled into Gil with his shoulder. Gil went down hard, and Brad was right on top of him. Brad's knees slipped over Gil's arms, pinning them to the ground, and Gil's face was a clear shot. Brad brought up his fist, and he saw it all, as though it were in slow motion. He could mash that face if he acted now—right now.

"That's it," he heard Theo say calmly, "he's all yours."

For a couple of seconds Brad looked down, and it was as though Gil were locked there, waiting for what was coming. But Brad saw the thing he had seen before in Gil's eyes. He couldn't hit him. Brad rolled off and jumped up. "Okay, now I know," he said to Theo.

"What do you know?"

"I saw how scared he was. He's just as scared as I am."

"So what?"

"I don't know. I . . . I don't really hate him."

There was a cracking noise, like something breaking, and suddenly Brad couldn't see. The light was too bright. He shut his eyes for a few seconds and then squinted to see what was happening. All around him was white, as though he were in a field of snow.

"Where am I? What's happening?"

"Don't let it scare you. It's just bright out here. We're on the salt flats."

"Salt flats? You mean out by the Great Salt Lake?"

"Of course."

"Why? What's going on?"

"Well, I have to leave now. I just wanted to take you somewhere where we could be alone and talk for a few minutes."

"Where are you going?"

"Away. It's what you wanted."

"You don't have to leave. I just wanted you not to do some of that stuff."

"I know. All the same, I do have to leave. But first tell me what you know. Make it into words."

"I told you. He's afraid too. I don't hate him anymore."

"You never did, Brad. But give me the rest of the words, so you won't forget them. Tell me what else you know."

"I guess we're all afraid at times."

"All right. That's very good. What made you see it finally?"

"I looked down at him, and it was like I was seeing myself."

"You've glimpsed. You've looked inside him and seen yourself. And now that you've had that glimpse, everything will start to change."

"But Theo, I'm not sure what I've glimpsed. I don't know where to go from there. I don't know everything."

"Don't say those words, Brad. You've only looked through a peephole, but everything is on the other side. A glimpse is almost everything. Now that you can see, keep looking."

"Theo, you never make anything easy."

"Quite the contrary. I need not have come at all."

"Are you going now?"

Theo nodded.

"Don't just disappear. Okay?"

"I won't. That's why I brought you out here. The horizon is far off."

"Won't I have you at all? Can't I think about you?"

"Brad, you know. Don't ask what you already know." Theo turned, as though he were about to walk away.

"What I think is real, isn't it?" Brad said.

Theo turned back around. He smiled. "The things you bump into—the stuff people call reality —don't mean very much. What you think is everything. You are what you think, Brad. Hate has more reality in it than a fist does."

Brad did understand that. He knew what damage his daydreams had been doing to himself, as well as to those around him. He felt he could let go now. "Good-bye, Bradley," he said.

"You're Bradley; I'm not. Not anymore. But remember, there was nothing wrong with making up a friend."

"I know. What was wrong was what I made you do. I let it all get out of control."

Theo nodded and then turned again.

"Theo, wait. You're not just the friend I made up. You're someone else too. Who are you?"

"I'm the Theo Zephyr. I'm the wind between time. When I come, I come as a gift. This time I was Bradley. But I don't always appear the same way."

"But why? Who sent you? Where do you come from?"

"It doesn't matter. What matters is what you know when I'm gone. I help people know what they know. Just remember that you looked inside Gil, your enemy, and you saw yourself. Build on that." He grinned, showing all those big teeth of his, and then he said, "Good-bye."

Brad nodded, but he couldn't speak. He felt the tears spill over on his cheeks as he watched Theo leave his life, pacing out across the whiteness of the salt flats. Theo's baggy pants rippled in the breeze, and his crazy hair flopped with each step.

Eventually Theo was only a speck, and still Brad watched in the waves of heat, trying to have one last moment of . . . and then the cracking sound again, and Brad was sitting at his desk in school.

The door had just opened. Everyone was looking up. They were supposed to be doing their math assignment, but it was Monday, and any interruption was welcome.

But no one was at the door. "The wind," someone said, and Brad thought that must be right, but as he looked around the room, he wondered what had happened. Everything looked different—*everything*.